OXFORD*classicPlayscripts*

○ ○

Doctor Faustus

Christopher Marlowe

adapted by

Geraldine McCaughrean

OXFORD
UNIVERSITY PRESS

OXFORD
UNIVERSITY PRESS

Great Clarendon Street, Oxford OX2 6DP

Oxford University Press is a department of the University of Oxford.
It furthers the University's objective of excellence in research,
scholarship, and education by publishing worldwide in

Oxford New York

Auckland Cape Town Dar es Salaam Hong Kong Karachi
Kuala Lumpur Madrid Melbourne Mexico City Nairobi
New Delhi Shanghai Taipei Toronto

With offices in

Argentina Austria Brazil Chile Czech Republic France Greece
Guatemala Hungary Italy Japan Poland Portugal Singapore
South Korea Switzerland Thailand Turkey Ukraine Vietnam

Oxford is a registered trade mark of Oxford University Press
in the UK and in certain other countries

This adaptation of **Doctor Faustus** © Geraldine McCaughrean 2005

Activity section © Jenny Roberts 2006

The moral rights of the author have been asserted

Database right Oxford University Press (maker)

This edition first published 2006

British Library Cataloguing in Publication Data

Data available

ISBN 978 0 19 832086 9

10 9 8 7 6 5 4 3 2

Typeset by Fakenham Photosetting Limited

Printed and bound by Bell and Bain Ltd, Glasgow.

Acknowledgements
Artwork is by Shirley Bellwood (B J Kearley Ltd.)
Engraving from Mary Evans Picture Library
Portrait from The Bridgeman Art Library

Dedication

For Rosie, Amy, Hazel and Otto

Contents

General Introduction

With a fresh, modern look, this classroom-friendly series boasts an exciting range of authors – from Pratchett to Chaucer – whose works have been expertly adapted by such well-known and popular writers as Philip Pullman and David Calcutt. We have also divided the titles available (see page 96) into subcategories – OXFORD *Classic Playscripts* and OXFORD *Modern Playscripts* – to make it even easier for you to think about titles – and periods – you wish to study.

Many teachers use OXFORD *Playscripts* to study the format, style, and structure of playscripts with their students; for speaking and listening assignments; to initiate discussion of relevant issues in class; to meet the Drama objectives of the Framework; as an introduction to the novel of the same title; and to introduce the less able or willing to pre-1914 literature.

At the back of each OXFORD *Playscript*, you will find a brand new Activity section, which not only addresses the points above, but also features close text analysis, and activities that provide support for underachieving readers and act as a springboard for personal writing. Furthermore, the new Activity sections now match precisely the Framework Objectives for Teaching English at Key Stage 3; a chart mapping the Objectives – and the activities that cover them – can be found at the beginning of each Activity section.

Many schools will simply read through the play in class with no staging at all, and the Activity sections have been written with this in mind, with individual activities ranging from debates and designing campaign posters to writing extra scenes or converting parts of the original novels into playscript form.

For those of you, however, who do wish to take to the stage, each OXFORD *Playscript* also features 'A Note on Staging' – a section dedicated to suggesting ways of staging the play, as well as examining the props and sets you may wish to use.

Above all, we hope you will enjoy using OXFORD *Playscripts*, be it on the stage or in the classroom.

About the Author

Christopher Marlowe was born in Canterbury in 1564, and is thought by many to be the greatest dramatist in England before Shakespeare. The son of a shoemaker, Marlowe was a talented student and earned a scholarship to study at the University of Cambridge. In 1587 he became an actor and playwright for the Lord Admiral's Company, and spent most of his career in London.

Marlowe's most important plays are *Tamburlaine the Great*, *Doctor Faustus*, *The Jew of Malta*, and *Edward II*. His plays often centre on one character who destroys himself through his own ambition and passion. *Tamburlaine*, the first of his plays to be performed on the London stage in 1587, was the first English play to make effective dramatic use of blank verse, and it marks the mature phase of Elizabethan Theatre.

As with other writers of the period, very little is known about Marlowe, but there has been much speculation on his activities and character. He is often regarded as a spy, a brawler, a heretic (holding beliefs contrary to Christianity) and a homosexual. Evidence of these claims is slight, hinted at in legal records and other official documents.

There is also some mystery surrounding his death. In early May 1953, bills were posted all over London threatening Protestant refugees who had settled in the city. One of these mentioned several of Marlowe's plays and was signed 'Tamburlaine'. On 11 May the Privy Council (a group of officials responsible for carrying out everyday government) ordered the arrest of those responsible for these bills, and the next day Marlowe's colleague Thomas Kyd was arrested. Kyd claimed, possibly under torture, that the evidence found in his lodgings belonged to Marlowe, and Marlowe's arrest was ordered on 18 May. Twelve days later, Marlowe was murdered in a bar-room brawl when he was stabbed above the right eye, killing him instantly. The coroner's inquest concluded that the culprit acted in self-defence, but it is likely that the murder had been planned. Since the available evidence is so sparse, we are unlikely to ever discover the full circumstances of Marlowe's death.

What the Adapter Says

Like the knife that stabbed Marlowe in the eye and killed him, scholars have been trying to penetrate the workings of his astonishing brain – to gouge out the innermost secrets of the man. As with Shakespeare (who imitated, then outshone him), facts about Marlowe's life are scarce: the son of a cobbler, he was exceptionally clever and probably a part-time spy. He was killed aged twenty-nine by a man who pleaded self-defence and was set free. If he had stayed alive for two more days Marlowe would have been arrested as an atheist.

An atheist? But *Doctor Faustus* is such a moral play! How could it possibly have been written by an atheist? Well, in Elizabethan times, 'atheism' did not mean not believing in God – it just meant not taking the Church's view of God.

Supposedly based on true events in Germany, the tale of Faustus was well known and popular in Marlowe's time, but had become a kind of knockabout farce – Punch and Judy, with the Devil in the place of the Policeman. Marlowe did so much more with the story. He kept in some farce, as a crowd pleaser, but Marlowe's Faustus sells his soul because he seeks knowledge and truth. There is nobility in his cause that almost wins us round. That is also where scholars glimpse Marlowe's atheism. I remember a church sermon I once attended, where the pen was named as the most dangerous weapon, because pens write down *ideas* and make people think for themselves instead of just trusting God to know best. In that moment I knew exactly what Marlowe and Faustus were about.

Marlowe is generally thought (but not known) to have been homosexual. In a famous speech in his original play about Helen of Troy, it is certainly striking that each instance of beauty he likens her to is masculine. So my version hints at a sort of love between Mephistopheles and Faustus, which intensifies their relationship. Other liberties I took as adapter mostly involve the dire sub-plots – but then some of those were not written by Marlowe.

Imagine writing a play at speed, and then having some mates add a few scenes, throwing the whole thing out of the window and the next day gathering up what's left. This was the puzzle facing academics analysing *Doctor Faustus*. Which words did Marlowe write? When were the extra bits added? By whom? What got lost? Why do sub-plots start and not finish; scenes repeat? What survived was an incomplete hotchpotch. You might want to adapt it yourself. Why not? Your new scenes would be just as valid as the ones put in after Marlowe's death (and probably better).

The fact remains that the best bits still have the power to make our hair stand on end. Imagine the impact they must have had on an audience to whom Hell was as real a place as Cambridge or Wapping.

The only thing I have deduced about Marlowe after adapting his play is that his imagination worked on a cosmic scale. He could, by words alone, cut a spy hole in the ordinary and let you see through to new heights, depths, and over the edge. While he wrote he got inside the characters and felt all their fear, regret, frustration, ambition and temptation. Be warned! That tells you nothing about what he personally believed – only that, at the moment of writing, an alchemical magic happened that transformed one young playwright, by turns, into angel, devil and death-defying genius.

A Note on Staging

The Play at a Glance

Faustus's study

Books hanging from above by chains; one book draped with black cloth; a Bible. Shelves lined with flasks, books, a pestle and mortar, a globe, stuffed animals. A high, clerk's writing desk with a pen and parchment. An hourglass; a penknife; chalk.

In Act 4, Scene 1, the following props can also be used: jug of wine; table heaped with food on plates, a carving knife and some glasses, chairs or a bench to seat five.

Papal Palace

A high, gilded throne sits centre back on the stage. Trestles, which will later hold a table top covered with a feast and napkins.

The court of Emperor Charles V

You can re-use the throne from the Papal Palace. There is a stepladder leading to a window.

The use of impact-detonating caps in some instances (mentioned in the stage directions) is optional.

Costumes and Props

Items you may need include:

Faustus	a friar's habit; a long black cloak; a false 'head' (for Act 3, Scene 4)
Wagner	a bag of gold
Bad Angel	a thunderboard; a noose; a dagger; poison; a gun
Mephistopheles	a friar's habit with knotted cord belt; a hank of hair; a bowl of cherries; two meat-hooks; a rag; a bone

Lucifer and **Beelzebub**	staffs (one each)
Anger	a rapier (thin, sharp-pointed sword)
Demon wife	shorts; apron; mobcap; mask; impact-detonating caps
Pope	a Triple Crown
Cardinals	a bell; a Bible; a tall, lit candle
Benvolio	antlers (wider than the window); a sword
King Darius	a golden crown
Helen of Troy	a veil
Devils	instruments of torture: blades; whips; hooks

Lighting and Sound Effects

Act 1

Scene 3   red light; thunder, lightning and smoke

Act 2

Scene 1   silhouettes of dragons against a backdrop; rungs of a ladder projected against the back wall in bright white light; thunder and lightning; the flicker of fire; disembodied screams

Act 3

Scene 2   amplified voice of Lucifer from offstage

Scene 3   trumpets

Scene 4   snare drums and marching feet; a church bell striking the hour

Act 4

Scene 1   a glass breaking; music; a clock striking the hour; red light; the words 'I Faustus' projected on the backdrop, possibly letter by letter

Scene 2   a clock projected against the backdrop; the sound of a clock ticking and striking the hours; smoke and the sound of roaring fire; red light; an hourglass almost run out projected against backdrop; thunder and lightning, smoke

Characters

The characters are listed in order of appearance and also stage set. Some of these are small parts and there are plenty of opportunities for doubling.

Dr Faustus's study

Faustus	An academic; has a big appetite for knowledge and power
Wagner	Faustus's servant; a student
Good Angel	
Bad Angel	
Valdes	} Faustus's friends; magicians
Cornelius	
Three students	
Mephistopheles	A devil
Robin	Wagner's friend; a simpleton
Chorus (four parts)	
Lucifer	
Beelzebub	A devil

The seven deadly sins:

> Pride
> Covetousness
> Envy
> Anger
> Gluttony
> Sloth
> Lechery

Demon wife	(non-speaking)
Rafe	Robin's friend; a simpleton and easily led

The Papal Palace

Demons	(non-speaking)
Pope	Pope Adrian; smug and unsympathetic
Bruno	The Emperor's 'chosen man'
Three Cardinals	

The court of Emperor Charles V

Martino
Frederick
Benvolio
Emperor   The Emperor of Germany, Charles V
Empress
Alexander the Great
King Darius   (non-speaking)
Roxane   (non-speaking)

An isolated spot

Asteroth   (non-speaking)
Belimoth   (non-speaking)

Old man

ACT 1

SCENE 1

Doctor Faustus's study.

Books hang by chains from above. One is draped with a black cloth. Shelves are lined with flasks, a pestle and mortar, a globe, stuffed animals. There is a high, clerk's writing desk.

Faustus wanders among the fruits of his varied studies.

Faustus Well, and where now? Here's where they all meet – all those paths to enlightenment I've travelled! This is the crossroads of my life! Which career shall I pursue to the utmost?

Thumbs through one of the books.

Philosophy? Treading in the footsteps of Aristotle and Plato? What's the purpose of philosophy? To reason with perfect logic. In short – to win any argument. Hmmm … Wagner!

Thumbs through another.

The Law! Shall I mete* out justice? Condemn the guilty? Free the innocent? Settle disputes? In short, win other people's

---

* mete – dispense or allot

arguments for them? What kind of calling is that? Pettifogging!* Wagner, come here!

Picks up and swirls various flasks.

Medicine, then. Shall I serve my fellow man by curing his ills? God knows, I can do it. I've saved whole cities from the plague before now. I might … except there's one ill I'll never cure. Sooner or later everyone dies. Healing is just staving off the inevitable – embalming the soon-to-be-dead. No. Not medicine. Wagner, where the devil are you?

Opens hanging Bible and points out texts to the audience.

Theology, then! To squeeze my thoughts through the narrow gate and down the thorny road to salvation! But look here: 'the wages of sin is death'. And yet here it says 'If we say we have no sin, we deceive ourselves'. So! How can we win? Not so much a road as a blind alley. And the clergy delight so in ignorance – suppress the ancient wisdoms; silence free thinkers; scowl on curiosity. Like nagging parents. All they ever say is *'No!'* No, no … I mean to open my mind, not close it!

He uncovers the book draped in black, suddenly becoming excited.

But this! Ah! This is the science that has me by the heartstrings! Magic! To harness magic and ride it over the world! To have spirits serve me like a staff of gardeners and skivvies! To whirl the stars around my head and stroll the heavens over bridges of cloud!

Copying from the book he chalks a pentacle onto the wall.

Yes! Forget the rest! I'll study necromancy**! [*Resting stretched hand on pentacle*] *This* is the star I'll pluck down!

*Enter **Wagner**, his servant.*

Wagner   Yes, master?

Faustus   Go and find Valdes and Cornelius. Ask them to call on me – the sooner the better.

* pettifogging – petty, trivial
** necromancy – witchcraft, sorcery, or black magic in general

Wagner	I will, sir.
	Exit Wagner.
Faustus	They're forever urging me to master the Black Arts. They've been dabbling for years. Their research can save me a deal of tedious study.
	Enter Good Angel from right, Bad Angel from left. Faustus cannot see them. He cradles the book lovingly. Good Angel tries to prise it out of his hands.
Good Angel	Stop! Think again. Don't open it, Faustus, if you value your soul! Those are secrets expressly forbidden to Man. Don't meddle with the powers of darkness. Read the scriptures instead! Your soul, Faustus – think of your soul!
	Bad Angel pulls the book free and opens it for Faustus.
Bad Angel	Do it, Faustus! All the wonders of Nature are in here, ready and awaiting your command! Hallowed be thy name on Earth as God's is in Heaven!
Faustus	And I could do such good by it! Build a brass wall right round Germany to protect her! I'll dress every student in silk! No one in all Wittenberg will go hungry! Oh and the spirits … my spirits! They'll answer all my questions. They'll finally satisfy this hunger in me to know how … where … who … why!
	Enter Cornelius and Valdes, brought in by Wagner, who makes to leave but hides instead.
	Cornelius! Valdes! Here you are! Come in. I want you to be the first to know. You've won me round. Of all the sciences I've ever studied, it's magic I've set my heart on.
Valdes	Faustus, with your genius and our experience, we'll have spirits flying to India for us daily to fetch back gold!
Faustus	*[Not quite listening to them]* Teaching us all the philosophies in the world!
Cornelius	Ransacking the oceans for pearls!
Faustus	Sharing the secrets of the universe!

Valdes	Searching the world over for strange delicacies!
Faustus	Singing us the music of the spheres!
Valdes	We'll be kings soon enough! With trains of spirits for our courtiers. What do you fancy for your escorts, Cornelius? *[Miming what he describes]* A pride of lions? A division of German cavalry? A couple of Lapland giants?
Cornelius	*[Miming what he describes]* Women! More beautiful than the Venus de Milo – and wearing less – waist deep in the ocean, towing treasure ships home from Venice stuffed with … That's if you really mean it …
Faustus	I mean it, Cornelius. Trust me, I mean it.
Cornelius	A little astrology, a few languages, a sprinkling of mineralogy … Add your genius and what *can't* we three do?
Faustus	Nothing! Oh my soul! Let's make a start!

Cornelius and Valdes select books and flasks from the shelves, then exit left.

I'll do it. Before I lay my head down tonight, I'll try my hand at magic. Damn me, but I will!

Exit Faustus left. Wagner emerges from hiding.

Wagner And damn me if I don't follow my 'worthy' master's example and study a little myself. They say a bit of learning is a dangerous thing, but it says here in this proverb 'A wise servant should have a share of the family fortune.' And who am I to argue with the Good Book?

Wagner sets the Bible spinning and exits left.

• •

SCENE 2

A street.

*Enter **two students** from right, **Wagner** from left.*

First student	There's his servant, look. We can ask him. You there!
Second student	Hey you! You're servant to Doctor Faustus, aren't you? He hasn't been seen around the university for weeks. Where is he?
Wagner	God knows.
First student	Why, don't *you* know, then?
Wagner	Oh yes, I know too.

*The **students** wait for an answer.*

| First student | Well? Are you going to tell us? |
| Wagner | He's out at dinner. With Valdes and Cornelius, magicians of this parish. If it's any of your business. |

***Wagner** revels in their shock and leaves.*

First student	The Black Arts!
Second student	I was afraid he might be toying with the idea. We must go and tell the Rector of the University. Perhaps he can help.
First student	I doubt that anyone can help Faustus now, if his heart is set on the occult!
Second student	We have to try, at least.

They exit right.

● ●

SCENE 3

Faustus's study.

*Enter **Faustus**. He starts chalking a circle on the ground.*

| Faustus | Now night's here … Now the dark has blindfolded the sun, let's put my new-found knowledge to the test. I've drawn all the constellations and symbols and words that force devils to show themselves. I've prayed to Lucifer … So! *[Chanting]* Hail spirits of fire, air and water! Who, for the sake of Lucifer, do fiery slaughter. |

Hail to the captain of your demon hoard!
Viceroy of Lucifer, my scarlet winged lord!
By hell, and holy water sprinkled here,
Mephistopheles I charge you to appear!

Pause.

What are you waiting for? Arise, Mephistopheles!

Thunder, light and smoke stream from offstage left but no one enters. **Faustus** *walks towards the source, sees something and screams. He covers his face and runs right to be sick.*

Too ugly! Change shape! I command you to come back in some other shape. You're too ugly to serve me!

Thunder and light stop. **Faustus** *recovers himself and giggles with hysteria.*

[*To audience*] You see? He obeys me! Oh! Who wouldn't master magic if he could? Poet laureate of incantations, that's me!

Meanwhile **Mephistopheles,** *dressed as a monk, walks up softly behind* **Faustus** *and touches him on the shoulder, making him jump.* **Mephistopheles** *is soft-spoken and agreeable.*

Mephistopheles	Yes, Faustus? What is it you want?
Faustus	[*Trying to hide his fear*] I c-c-command you to wait on me!

Pause as **Faustus** *waits for a refusal, but none comes.*

All life long.

Another pause.

To do whatever I tell you.

Another pause.

Whatever – even if I want the Moon to drop out of the sky or the ocean to swamp the land!

Mephistopheles	[*Raising hands to cast a spell*] Oceans …
Faustus	NO! Not just now!

Mephistopheles	I am a servant to the great Lucifer. I cannot serve you unless he grants his permission.
Faustus	But he must have sent you. Here, I mean – just now.
Mephistopheles	No. I came of my own accord.
Faustus	*[Crestfallen]* Didn't my magic raise you?
Mephistopheles	In a manner of speaking. Whenever we spirits hear a man trying to bring down damnation on himself, we hurry close in the hope of his soul. Like dogs at feeding time.
Faustus	Damnation? Ha! I don't believe in it any more than the Greeks did. Now I've perfected my studies, I intend to build a Heaven for myself right over the ruins of Hell … Tell me about Lucifer. I want to know. I want to know everything!
Mephistopheles	Lucifer. Ruler of Evil. Commander of us spirits.
Faustus	Wasn't he an angel once?
Mephistopheles	God's right-hand man. His dearest companion. He was thrown down from Heaven for plotting rebellion – for treachery.
Faustus	And you?
Mephistopheles	One of the unhappy spirits who fell with Lucifer; conspired against God with Lucifer; am forever damned with Lucifer.

Faustus clumsily gestures the Fall and where *Mephistopheles* landed.

Faustus	But where? Where did you fall … I mean, where do you … I mean, to where …
Mephistopheles	To Hell.
Faustus	In that case, how are you out of Hell now? Here, with me?
Mephistopheles	Why this is Hell, nor am I out of it. Do you suppose that I – who have seen the face of God and the perpetual bliss of Heaven – do not suffer ten thousand kinds of Hell knowing they are lost to me forever?

> *Mephistopheles sinks down, curls into a foetal agony and weeps, while **Faustus** looks on, baffled. At last **Mephistopheles** rises again, passing a hand in front of his face and adopting a broad smile, as if the outburst was a joke.*

Faustus　　　　Take this message to your master – to Lucifer – and say that Faustus will surrender his soul in return for … for twenty-four years of my heart's desire. Tell him I want you for my squire – to come when I call; do everything I ask; kill my enemies; help my friends. Come back here at midnight with his answer.

Mephistopheles　　I will, Faustus.

> *Exit **Mephistopheles**.*

Faustus　　　　*[Triumphant]* If I had as many souls as there are stars in the sky, I'd give them all to have this Mephistopheles serve me! He'll make me Emperor of the World! I've done it!

> *He sets an hourglass running.*

What a dreary long time to wait! But then, midnight! And Mephistopheles again!

● ●

SCENE 4

> *A street.*

> *Enter **Wagner** and his friend, **Robin**, laughing.*

Robin　　　　　Doesn't it worry you – what people are saying about your master?

Wagner　　　　Why should it? People jump out of our way whenever we walk down the street. The tradesmen are too scared to demand payment. Even the dogs don't dare bite Faustus. Anyway, I know you! You'd sell your soul to the Devil for a joint of raw mutton.

Robin　　　　　I would not!

Wagner　　　　Would, too!

Robin	Would not! … I'd want it cooked first!
Wagner	Me, I could keep you in roast mutton all your days, with what I know.
Robin	Really?
Wagner	Want to be my servant and work for me?
Robin	*[Doing monkey impression]* What for, peanuts?

Wagner produces a bag of gold.

Wagner	I was thinking more of this.
Robin	*[Clutching his chest]* Ooh! I think I've just had a change of heart! Give it here! Let me feel that lovely … Where did you get this kind of money?
Wagner	So now you're my servant, you must go wherever I send you and do whatever I command.
Robin	But you're a servant yourself!
Wagner	I'm delegating.
Robin	*[Becoming serious]* How did you get hold of money like this, Wagner?
Wagner	I can have all I want, just by asking. That's what you get for serving a master of the Black Arts.
Robin	*[Realizing what he means]* Here. Take your money back. I don't want it.
Wagner	*[Shaking his head]* You took it. That's a contract.
Robin	I'm breaking it. Nothing would induce me to serve a man in league with the Devil.
Wagner	*[Menacing]* Nothing? What, not even a couple of demons summoned up from Hell to kick you from here to Hallowe'en? Come Baliol! Come Beltcher! Good. I hear them coming now.

Sobbing, Robin hides, wrapping himself in the curtains which tremble violently. No demons appear.

Robin	All right, all right! I'll serve you! Keep them off me, Wagner!
Wagner	You can come out now.
Robin	*[Emerging fearfully]* Have they really gone?
Wagner	I told them to come back another time. If I need them. Cheer up, servant. If you behave yourself, I'll teach you how to change yourself into a dog … or a rat, even!
Robin	I'd settle for being turned into the man I was before. Before I took that money.
Wagner	Baliol! Beltcher!
Robin	No, no! Shush! Don't! I'll serve you, Wagner. I will!
Wagner	*Master* Wagner, if you please. And you'll walk ten steps behind me at all times, and only speak when you're spoken to.
	Exit Wagner left.
Robin	*[Trailing behind]* God forgive me. I'd rather have signed up to wrestle crocodiles stark naked.
Wagner	*[Off]* Baliol! Beltcher!
Robin	Coming, master! Sorry, master!
	Exit Robin.

● ●

SCENE 5

Faustus's study.

Faustus paces anxiously. The hourglass is almost empty. He collides with the Bible hanging by its chain.

Faustus Damnation! *Must* I be damned, then? Is there nothing for it? *[Pause]* No point in brooding, then. On God, or Heaven. Cut God adrift and put all my faith in the Devil. *[Pause]* Come on, Faustus. No turning back. No looking over your shoulder. This is no time to lose your nerve.

*Enter **Good Angel** from right. It is invisible to **Faustus**.*

Good Angel It is *just* the time, Faustus. Repent! Pray! Beg forgiveness! Turn to God again!

Faustus *[Without acknowledging the angel]* God doesn't love me. I don't believe He ever did. Anyway, He hates me now, that is certain.

Good Angel No, no! Isn't God the very stuff of Love? Isn't His love without limit? Can't He forgive anyone? Anything?

*Enter **Bad Angel** from left, also invisible to **Faustus**.*

Bad Angel Forgive a man who has made a god of his own selfishness? God's love is an illusion; wishful thinking. Do you want to be one of those fools who spends his life mumbling superstitious excuses to a deaf god?

Good Angel Sweet Faustus, think of Heaven! Think of heavenly things!

Bad Angel Think of Wealth! Think of Power! Think of Knowledge!

*Exit **Angels**.*

Faustus What can God do to me anyway, with Mephistopheles at my shoulder? I'm safe. Oh, come on, Mephistopheles! Isn't it midnight yet? *Veni, Mephistophele!* Tell me what answer Lucifer sends!

*Again, **Mephistopheles** enters silently, creeping up behind **Faustus** and tapping him on the shoulder, making him jump.*

Mephistopheles That I shall serve Faustus for as long as he lives … Providing he pays with his soul.

Faustus	I've already said I will. I do!
Mephistopheles	These things must be done properly. There must be a deed of gift.

Faustus readily goes to the desk and picks up a pen and parchment.

Written in blood.

Faustus falters.

If you refuse, I'm gone. Back to Hell.

Mephistopheles makes to leave.

Faustus	Wait! Don't go! Tell me … What good will my one little soul do your master?
Mephistopheles	*[Shrugging]* It will enlarge his kingdom.
Faustus	But why –
Mephistopheles	It is a comfort, when you're suffering torment, to know that others are sharing your pain.
Faustus	You suffer pain? You demons?
Mephistopheles	As much as those we torment.

Mephistopheles's face, turned towards the audience, is a mask of pain and unhappiness.

Let us talk on other matters. Well? Am I to grant your wishes? All of them? Even those you haven't the wit to ask for?

Faustus picks up a penknife but can't make the cut. Mephistopheles comes and takes the knife hand tenderly between his own, looking into Faustus's eyes.

One little cut. A moment's pain. One little soul. Twenty-four years of joy. Then Lucifer will come and take you to him. *[Embracing Faustus]* And you will be Lucifer's equal in happiness!

He kisses Faustus on the cheek. Faustus stabs himself in the arm.

Red light washes the whole stage. Mephistopheles breaks sharply away.

Faustus	See what I've done for your sake, Mephistopheles?

He tries to charge his quill with blood.

Oh! But it keeps congealing! Why won't it run? Does my own body shrink from making this bargain?

Mephistopheles returns and chafes Faustus's hands to increase the circulation.

Mephistopheles	*[Aside]* What won't I do to have this one man's soul?
Faustus	It is done! It's written! 'I, John Faustus of Wittenberg, in return for that I ask, do solemnly swear to give up body and soul to Lucifer, Prince of Darkness, after the space of twenty-four years. So help me, G– *[Correcting himself]* Mephistopheles. *[Revulsion]* Look how the veins of my arm are coiling and knotting themselves into letters … words! Run, Faustus! Run? Where? Where can I run?
Mephistopheles	Something to console my … master.

He claps his hands and two devils enter carrying a golden cloak and a crown. Mephistopheles helps Faustus to put them on.

Faustus	*[Admiring himself]* Is this how it will be, then?
Mephistopheles	This and more.
Faustus	*[Suddenly doubtful]* You haven't just tricked me into …
Mephistopheles	I swear, Faustus. I will keep my side of the bargain. I will serve you, empower you, obey and instruct you. So help me Lucifer.
Faustus	I think Hell's a fable.
Mephistopheles	Good for you. Cling on to that thought, until experience teaches you differently.

Mephistopheles makes to go.

Faustus	*[Arrogant]* Why? Do you think I will be damned, then?

Mephistopheles, astounded by **Faustus**'s stupidity, simply holds up the scroll in reply. Exit both.

ACT 2

● ●

SCENE 1

Faustus's study.

A blank backdrop obscures the shelves and apparatus.

*Enter **Chorus**. Their shadows are cast tall behind them, then they step aside and silhouettes of dragons swoop across the backdrop.*

Chorus 1	Eight days. Eight little days, and Faustus viewed the Earth from end to end. Mounted astride dragons he and Mephistopheles swooped beneath the pale arctic sun, casting fantastical shadows on glaciers and snowfields untrodden by Man.
Chorus 2	Their saddles slippery with sweat, they followed the Equator round the great girth of the Earth, slipped through the shining tunnels of curling tidal waves and dodged the pluming lava of volcanoes.

Chorus 3	Deserts furrowed like God's brow. Jungles as teeming with strangeness as the mind of God.
Chorus 4	They careered as low as the River Styx and the caves of Morpheus where nightmares hang from the roofs like bats; saw the sweating walls of iron that surround the realm of Hell.
Chorus (all)	Heard the sounds from inside.
Chorus 1	But though they flogged their dragon mounts as high as Heaven, the shining shield of light rebuffed them, impenetrable. Like fish butting their noses against the ice of a frozen pond, they could not rise into the realm of light.
Chorus 2	Impossible that Mephistopheles, banished forever from Heaven, should find his way back in.
Chorus 3 & 4	Impossible that Faustus, his soul sold to Lucifer, should ever glimpse the God he had foresworn.

*The backdrop rises, returning us to **Faustus**'s study.*

***Faustus** enters, pushing **Mephistopheles** roughly onstage ahead of him. He is richly dressed and looks younger, but is twitchy with anxiety. **Mephistopheles** is infinitely patient and calm, but suffers physical pain every time God or Heaven is mentioned.*

Faustus	Curse you, Mephistopheles! You've robbed me! Robbed me!
Mephistopheles	What can you mean, Faustus? Every day I bring you money and possessions and sensual delights.
Faustus	I mean Heaven, you fiend! You've robbed me of Heaven! Every time I look up at the sky I remember what I lost when I signed up to your villainous bargain.
Mephistopheles	Don't trouble yourself about Heaven. I tell you, Faustus, Heaven is nothing in comparison with you.
Faustus	Is that so? And how do you argue that?
Mephistopheles	It was made for Mankind, wasn't it? So it stands to reason Mankind is more wonderful than Heaven.

Faustus	If Heaven was made for Mankind, it was made for me. I'll give up this Magic and repent!
	*Faustus falls to his knees and tries to pray. Enter **Good Angel** from right, **Bad Angel** from left, carrying a thunderboard.*
Good Angel	Yes, yes, Faustus! That's right! God will take pity on you!
Bad Angel	*[Shaking the thunderboard over **Faustus's** head]* You're half demon already, Faustus. How can God ever pity a devil like you?
Faustus	I can't think! I can't shape my thoughts into prayers! I go to speak the words 'salvation', 'sorry', 'sinner', and my head fills up with thunder!
	*Bad Angel produces, one by one, a noose, a dagger, poison, a gun, and tries to tempt **Faustus** to commit suicide.*
	End it, then, Faustus! Do away with yourself! What point is there in going on living, tormented by the thought of what's to come?
Good Angel	Do not despair! You *mustn't* despair, Faustus!
Faustus	No. Why should I? There's such sweetness and beauty …
Good Angel	Well said, Faustus! That's right! Take courage! Fix your eyes on -
Faustus	I have Magic, don't I? Magic can banish the deepest, blackest despair! I've done it a thousand times. Haven't I, Mephistopheles? Haven't I?
	*Action freezes and the backdrop descends again, as **Chorus** enters. Some of what they describe is projected against the backdrop in silhouette.*
Chorus 1	So he has. Faustus has plundered the past for moments of perfection.
Chorus 2	He has heard the poet Homer sing love songs under a Mediterranean sky.
Chorus 3	He has heard the musician Amphion play his lyre – a sound so

beautiful that the stones heaved themselves up from the ground to form the shining walls of Thebes.

Chorus 4	To satisfy his curiosity he has harnessed a burnished chariot and, with Mephistopheles for his charioteer, careered across the Milky Way, and swung in the crescent sliver of a new moon to view the planets and the stars.
Chorus 3	Visited the various wonders of the world.

*Meanwhile, **Mephistopheles** cuts and folds newspaper into a paper chain of people.*

Chorus 2	Far more than seven.
Chorus 1	Far, *far* more than seven.
Chorus (all)	Numberless wonders …
Faustus	And all mine for the asking! No! I don't repent anything! Mephistopheles, tell me more about the universe.
Mephistopheles	Nine planets circle the sun, each fixed in its looping orbit, each revolving on its own axis. But since they turn at different speeds, a year on Jupiter lasts twelve times longer than –
Faustus	Yes, yes, I know. Everyone knows about the workings of the Solar System! Wagner could have told me that! Tell me something I don't know! Tell me, what … what's beyond the Universe?
Mephistopheles	Nothing.
Faustus	What, no realms of fire and crystal?
Mephistopheles	No, that's just hearsay.
Faustus	And who made the world?

Mephistopheles is silent.

I asked you a question. Who made the world? Tell me!

Mephistopheles	No, I will not.
Faustus	Villain! Haven't I commanded you to tell me everything I want to know?

Mephistopheles	Do not press me, Faustus.
Bad Angel	Forget the world, Faustus. Think about Hell instead.
Good Angel	Think about Heaven, Faustus – and God. It was He who made the world!

Mephistopheles covers his ears and leaves in a hurry, left.

Faustus	Yes, go! Go on! Get back to Hell, you damned demon! You've stolen the soul out of me! It's not too late, though, is it?
Bad Angel	Much too late.
Good Angel	*Never* too late. Not if you are truly sorry!
Bad Angel	Repent and a thousand demons will burst out of Hell to tear you to shreds.
Good Angel	Repent and they won't be able to touch one hair on your head!

Faustus falls to his knees, clasped hands upraised.

Projected on the back wall in bright white light are the rungs of a ladder descending to within reach, though Faustus's eyes are shut.

Look up, Faustus! Faustus, look –

Bad Angel clamps a hand over Good Angel's mouth and they wrestle to ensure that Faustus sees/does not see the ladder.

Faustus	Oh Christ my Saviour, save my –

Thunder, lightning, the flicker of fire, disembodied screams. Enter Lucifer and Beelzebub, fetched urgently by Mephistopheles. The ladder disappears. They circle Faustus.

Beelzebub	Faustus! You break the terms of your contract! You call on … names you should have forgotten by now.
Faustus	*[Terrified]* I'm sorry!
Beelzebub	You should think on the Devil.
Faustus	Yes, yes. I will! I do!
Beelzebub	And his wife.

Faustus	I'll never do it again! I'll never name God or Christ!

The devils flinch at the words as if burned by them.

	Or Heaven or Salvation! I'll tell my demons to pull down churches and burn the Scriptures! *[Pause]* His wife?
Beelzebub	We will reward you for it.
Faustus	The Devil has a wife?
Mephistopheles	How would you care for an audience with the Seven Deadly Sins? Wouldn't that amuse you?
Faustus	As much as seeing Adam and Eve naked in the Garden of Eden!

Again, the devils flinch.

Beelzebub	*[To Mephistopheles]* Can't you stop him doing that?
Mephistopheles	I'll do my best to divert him. Behold, Faustus! For your delectation and delight, The Seven Deadly Sins, who, like a reef of rocks, catch at the kneels of god-fearing men and sink their souls to perdition.*

*Enter **Pride** from left (as do all the sins in turn), posturing, looking about and sniffing contemptuously.*

Pride	What kind of a place is this for someone of my breeding?
Faustus	Who are you?
Pride	I am Pride, of course. Who else? I am the feather fan kissing the face of a vain young woman. I am the ruff round the throat of the fashionable young fop.** I am the sneer on the face of the arrogant banker. I am the gloat in the throat of the winning scholar. I am *far* too important to be speaking to the likes of you. And this place smells. I won't say another word until you sprinkle some perfume and lay down a few tapestries for me to walk on. The soles of my shoes are getting dirty.
Faustus	Pride in person, it's true!

* perdition – (in Christian theology) a state of eternal punishment and damnation after death
** fop – a man who is overly concerned with his clothes and appearance

*Enter **Covetousness** sizing up the contents of **Faustus**'s study, fingering everything – his clothing, hair, desk.*

Covetousness If I just had your brains I'd have devils to wait on me as well. What did you do to get those boots? Nothing honest, I'll swear. It's just not fair! If I had your luck, I'd be clever, too. And famous! We're not all as fortunate as Faustus, you know. Ooh, if I had this house, I'd lock it away safe in here *[Clutching his chest]* and never show it to anyone. They only rob you, people.

Faustus Are you Covetousness or Envy?

*Enter **Envy**, whining and morose. **Faustus** has to restrain **Envy** from destroying things.*

Envy *[Whining]* He is Covetousness. I am Envy. I can't read, so I want all the books in the world piled up in bonfires and burned. Everyone has more than I do. May plague and famine rot the lot of you! Everyone's got more to eat than me – better clothes, more friends. That chariot outside – what did you ever do to deserve that? Some people have all the luck. Hate them. And how's this? You're sitting, and I'm standing up. Ugh, it's so unfair!

Faustus Next!

*Enter **Anger**, his belt stuffed with daggers, lashing out with a rapier* and throwing his fists about so that everyone – sins, devils, **Faustus** – has to duck. **Anger** grabs **Faustus** by the lapels and drags him close, nose-to-nose.*

Anger What are you looking at? You make me want to spit blood, your sort. You shouldn't be let loose! You're disgusting. I was born in a lion's mouth – jumped out of it when I was an hour old, like a roar in a nappy. Been looking for your kind ever since, to slice up and eat raw. You make me want to vomit. Hell's teeth, you'll be sorry if you ever get in my way again!

*Rages offstage left, colliding with **Gluttony** (who enters) and pummeling him/her for getting in the way.*

* rapier – a thin, sharp-pointed sword used for thrusting

Gluttony is grossly fat and always talking with a full mouth. He/she grabs food first, then candles, quills, buttons, and handkerchiefs, cramming them into his/her mouth.

Gluttony   Spare me a guilder, gentlemen, for the love of roast pork! My parents are dead and they only left me enough money for thirty meals a day and ten snacks. My father was a side of bacon and my mother was a barrel of beer, and look at me! Wasting away for want of a square meal! Will you invite me to supper, Faustus? I'm wonderful company! Sharp as a lemon! *[Belches]*

Faustus   Not for all the oranges in Seville. You'd eat me out of house and home. Go on. Get out.

Gluttony   Devil choke you, then.

Faustus   He won't need to trouble choking you. You'll do that yourself. Who's this coming?

Sloth drags him/herself onstage and slumps heavily against Faustus, yawning.

Well then? Are you going to tell me who you are?

After lengthy consideration, Sloth sighs and shakes his/her head.

Everyone   Sloth.

Faustus   So what are you good for, my fine idle gentleman?

Sloth   *[Yawning]* For a long afternoon on a sunny bank. For a Sunday morning free of churchgoing. For an excuse to let the world go hang itself. *[Trailing off]* Got fetched here ... was sunbathing ... doing nothing ... go disturbing people ... shouldn't be allowed.

Faustus   Go on, then. Get back there and continue doing what you were not.

Sloth   Someone has to carry me ... you ... you ...

Enter Lechery, a woman dressed to kill, but unsavoury and slightly grubby.

Faustus   *[Whistling softly]* And who are *you*?

*Lechery seductively sits on **Faustus**'s lap and tousles his hair. She is raunchy and suggestive.*

Lechery	I'm the one who wants whatever you have to give, lover, and the more the better. I can solve all your problems, Doctor; nothing is too difficult for me. Let me spell my name for you and then I'll have you under my spell. L is for lust, E is for excess, C is for clinging close; H is for hot; E is for …
Faustus	*[Laughing and dropping her on the floor]* Oh no! A spell of Lechery can seriously damage a man's marriage prospects. Away to Hell with you … to Hell with you all!

*Exit the remaining deadly sins, **Gluttony** and **Covetousness** carrying **Sloth**.*

Lucifer	Well, Faustus? Did this little entertainment of ours please you?
Faustus	By God it did!

*The devils flinch and growl but **Faustus** is too preoccupied to notice.*

Beelzebub	*[To **Mephistopheles**]* Can't you stop him doing that?
Lucifer	Fix your thoughts on the Devil, Faustus!

*Exit **Lucifer**.*

Beelzebub	And on his wife!

*Exit **Beelzebub**.*

Faustus	*[Watching them leave, distractedly]* Talking of marriage prospects … I should like a wife, Mephistopheles. I have a hankering to be married. Find me a wife, Mephistopheles: a beautiful, accomplished, heart-stopping wife!
Mephistopheles	Marriage, Faustus? What do you want with a wife? A fig for wives!

***Faustus** is amused, as he mistakes **Mephistopheles**'s uneasiness for jealousy.*

Faustus	Even so, sweet Mephistopheles, fetch me one. I will have a wife. Now, Mephistopheles! In accordance with our bargain?

*There is a momentary stand-off between them. **Mephistopheles** appears to lose.*

Mephistopheles	A wife, then. Sit there while I fetch you a wife *[Aside]* in the devil's name.

He 'draws' a door in the wall, which then magically opens. A lewd male demon leaps from the door, grotesquely dressed in shorts, apron, mob cap and mask. The demon wife throws down impact-detonating caps at **Faustus**'s feet and chases him around the stage.*

	Well? What do you think of her?
Faustus	Take her away, the hag! Is that the best you can do?

***Mephistopheles** dismisses the demon wife who stumps off explosively.*

Mephistopheles	*[Smoothing him down]* By no means, Faustus! By no means! I can bring you the loveliest women in the world – white as sea foam or black as the lightless ocean bed. Their likenessess, anyway. A new one every day. As tender as a doe or as fierce as a tiger. A woman to suit your every mood. Faustus need never be lonely. *[Aside]* But why marry any of them? Forget marrying! Marriage – it's nothing but a meaningless ceremony for shackling a man to his mistakes …

*There is a momentary stand-off. This time **Mephistopheles** has won.*

Faustus	Thank you for your advice.
Mephistopheles	*[Distracting him like a child]* I have a book here, you may care to see. It shows how you may summon the elements of thunder, wind, storm and lightning.
Faustus	Truly?
Mephistopheles	And strong men. In harnesses. Ready to obey your every command.
Faustus	What I would really like is a book that shows –
Mephistopheles	*[Producing a book by magic]* And here it is!
Faustus	But how could you possibly know –
Mephistopheles	Haven't I served my Faustus long enough to anticipate his every thought?

* mob cap – a large soft hat covering all of the hair and typically having a
decorative frill, worn indoors by women in the 18th and early
19th centuries

They leave, trust and friendship restored between them. Enter
Robin *through the new door, bewildered by it being there. He looks*
around shiftily, then, seeing a book on the desk, takes it and leaves.

ACT 3

SCENE 1

In front of drawn curtains (Papal Palace behind).

Enter **Robin**, *clutching the stolen book and looking very pleased*
with himself.

Robin I've stolen one of the Doctor's magic books! So who's the
magician now, Master Wagner? I'll be able to work all manner
of magic! *[He starts to chalk on the ground]* I'll be famous for
my wisdom just like Faustus is now! Kings and Emperors will
invite me to Court same as they do the Mighty Faustus, just to
hear the wisdom spilling from my head. No more fetching and
carrying for Wagner. No more licking of his boots!

He struts about, performing various occult-looking contortions and
rummaging through the book for spells.

Enter a friend, **Rafe**, *behind him.* **Rafe** *is a bumpkin and easily*
led; he is curious to know what is going on. He bends round and
over **Robin**, *watching what he is doing. He taps him on the*
shoulder, making him jump.

Robin Avaunt* thee, Satan! Oh it's you, Rafe. Get away! Move off
out of here! You don't want to be here when I do my magic.
There's roaring work going on hereabouts! I've got a *book*!

Rafe *[Scoffing] You* can't read!

Robin Can too!

Rafe Can not!

Robin Can too! Watch here! What's your pleasure? I'll have all the

35

* avaunt – go away

women in Wittenberg falling down stark naked at your feet. I'll have all the landlords fetching us beer by the barrel and paying *us* to drink it!

Rafe Never!

Robin I'll have my horse live on fresh air for a year and never have to buy hay, nor oats – not once in a twelvemonth! Eat your soul out, Wagner! I'll have twenty demons to your two! Then we'll see who's servant and who's master!

Rafe You can do all that with a book? I wish I'd learned to read!

Robin Stand back! And prepare to be amazed! Polyparrot Beelzepoppin matelosan rentawenchies costalot Lucifurry bubblegluggin tostu Mephistopheles –

*Enter **Mephistopheles** amidst the sound of thunder, in a towering rage, holding the pope's Triple Crown.*

*O mea culpa. Mea culpa!**

Rafe *O misericordia pro nobis!*****

Mephistopheles Villains! Amateurs! You meddling fools have fetched me from the job in hand and brought me all the way here from Rome!

Robin *[Trying a bribe]* Rome, did you say? That's quite a journey. Would you take sixpence to buy yourself some supper?

Rafe I reckon he's more than sixpence-worth angry, Robin.

Mephistopheles I'll teach you to dabble in the damned arts! I'll dance you to Damascus and back for your damned magic!

Mephistopheles *throws down impact-detonating caps at their feet.*

I'll turn *you* into an ape … and *you* into a dog. I'll damn you up hill and down dale! Twenty demons, did you say? I'll give you twenty demons! *Do it, demons, and damn them!*

*Lots of demons rush across the stage from left to right and chase **Rafe** and **Robin** offstage. **Mephistopheles** storms out again the opposite way. Curtains draw back to reveal the Papal Palace, Rome.*

---

* *Mea culpa!* – My fault!
** *misericordia pro nobis!* – Pity for us!

SCENE 2

The Papal Palace, Rome. A high, gilded throne sits centre back on the stage. Trestles stand ready to receive the table top in due course.

Faustus stands gazing around him in awe which implies the splendour of the place. Mephistopheles skids onstage still muttering with anger and carrying a friar's habit like the one he wears. He thrusts it at Faustus.

Mephistopheles   Fools! Amateurs! Put on this friar's habit, my Faustus. Then not only can you watch the Feast of Saint Peter, you can play a part in the farce too. *[Afterthought]* If you wish.

Faustus   *[Putting on the habit]* Of course, of course! But look around, Mephistopheles! What beauty! What grandeur! Works of art at every turn!

Mephistopheles   Luxury, opulence, wanton* extravagance … So *marvellously* in keeping with vows of poverty.

Faustus   Ah. Yes, hmm.

Mephistopheles   This is the den of Germany's enemies. Remember, this Pope Adrian has seized the Emperor's chosen man, Bruno, and dragged him in chains to Rome. But Faustus wished to come, so here we are – *[with mischievous relish]* to play our part in the solemnities.

Faustus   Yes, humour me, sweet Mephistopheles. I want to use every single hour and afternoon and day and week filling my head with sights and scenes – feeding my store of knowledge! Increasing my understanding!

Mephistopheles   *[Aside]* And on tomfoolery, of course.

Faustus   Sights that ravish the eye; encounters that enrich the soul …

Mephistopheles   *[Aside]* And jesting, naturally. *[To Faustus]* Into character, now, my Faustus. The procession is coming.

*Grandiose organ music. Enter the **Pope** and his **Cardinals**, then **Bruno** in chains. He is forced to kneel while the **Pope** uses him as a step to his throne. The **Pope** is smug, shrill and unsympathetic.*

* wanton – luxuriant

37

Pope	Thus will we set our foot on the necks of all dissenters! German Bruno, your life is forfeit and your soul, too. We excommunicate you from the grace of God.
Bruno	I protest! I will be heard! Grant me right of trial! I was appointed by the Emperor himself!
Pope	Then we excommunicate the Emperor too!
Bruno	But Pope Julian – who passed down to you that papal Triple Crown you wear – promised Rome would always honour the Emperor's decrees!
Pope	Then we excommunicate Pope Julian too! Take him away!
Faustus	Insufferable tyrant! Come, friend. We'll escort his prisoner for him – directly out of Rome.
	Faustus and Mephistopheles step reverently up to the throne as if to escort the prisoner, and urge Bruno towards the edge of the stage.
Pope	Wait!
	A tense pause while it remains uncertain if the Pope has realized that Faustus and Mephistopheles are intruders. The Pope takes off his Triple Crown.

Take this crown to my apartments. It weighs too heavy for the sport of eating, and I dare say my brains will be sore enough by the end of the Feast of Saint Peter. *[Rubbing his hands in greedy glee]*

Faustus	*[Going back for the crown; aside]* By Lucifer, this is turning out better than I could have hoped!
Mephistopheles	Well enough … *[Aside]* for a pantomime.

*Exit **Faustus** and **Mephistopheles** with **Bruno**.*

Pope	Bring in the Feast!

*Enter six servants carrying a table top spread with meat, cakes, and fruit, which they place on its trestles. The **Pope** and **Cardinals** all produce napkins which they tuck into their collars.*

*Re-enter **Faustus** and **Mephistopheles** front left without their habits. They are 'invisible', so go unnoticed, despite the fact that **Faustus** is now wearing the Triple Crown on his head.*

Faustus	Bruno is free of his chains and safely spirited out of Rome! And not five minutes have passed! Where's this spiteful tyrant's triumph now? Trickled away like the sand through an hourglass! Are we truly invisible, then?
Mephistopheles	You took off your solid shape along with your friar's habit. Now you are free to 'partake' of the Pope's hospitality, with or without a dinner invitation. Go on. Show this glutton how Faustus can pick the lock on his larder!

*As the **Pope** and **Cardinals** pass each other food, invisible **Faustus** intercepts it, steals it from between their very teeth, drinks their wine between it being poured and sipped.*

*Mephistopheles also snatches the food out of their hands and the throne from under the **Pope** as he leans forward for food (though **Mephistopheles** does not himself eat or express real mirth).*

Pope	*[Shrill and scared]* Saucy spirits! Impious ghosts! Thieving demons! Fetch the instruments of excommunication! Someone must be damned for this before I starve!

*Exit three **Cardinals**, running.*

Mephistopheles	*[With mock horror]* Oh Faustus! Now you'll be damned with bell, book and candle, for stealing the Pope's supper! Whatever will you do?
Faustus	*[Giggling]* Bell book and candle, candle book and bell, forward and backward, let them curse Faustus to Hell!
	Cardinals return, one with a bell, one with a Bible, one with a tall lit candle.
Cardinal with bell	*[Chanting and ringing bell]* Cursed be he who stole his Holiness's meat! *Maledicat dominus!**
Cardinal with bible	*[Chanting, then turning the Bible upside down]* Cursed be he who drank his Holiness's wine! *Maledicat dominus!*
Cardinal with candle	*[Chanting]* Cursed be he who caught his Holiness a blow on the ear! *Maledicat domin* – oh!
	Faustus jumps forward playfully and blows out the candle himself.
Mephistopheles	*[To himself]* Brave Faustus – so eager to sink himself in the dark.
	*Having achieved his various ends, **Mephistopheles** throws impact-detonating caps among the **Pope** and **Cardinals**, causing them to scatter. **Mephistopheles** and **Faustus** chase them offstage, **Faustus** jeering and tripping them up.*
	*Enter **Chorus**. The curtain draws behind them to allow a scene change.*
Chorus (all)	Brave Faustus.
Chorus 1	His sights set upon fame and enlightenment. He steals a bite of bread, a slurp of wine …
Chorus 2	… blows out a candle, too, and with it his right to the bread and wine of Communion, the flesh and blood of Christ.
Chorus 3	Even so his fame *has* spread, his fame is spreading still. Back in Wittenberg his fellow scholars welcome him home open-armed.
Chorus 4	Shower him with questions. Wonder at his wit.

* *Maledicat dominus!* – May the Lord curse him!

Chorus 3	Faustus is famous. Faustus is honoured world wide.
Chorus (all)	Even in Hell his name resounds, as the years pass … and the years pass, and the years run down like sand.

Exit **Chorus.**

Voice of **Lucifer,** *hugely amplified, calls teasingly.*

Lucifer	Faustus! Oh Faustus! *We cannot wait to have you here with us!*

● ●

SCENE 3

The court of Emperor Charles V.

The papal throne is now the **Emperor's.** *There is a stepladder to one side, leading up to a window facing out towards the audience.* **Benvolio** *is propped up against the window sill, sleeping off a night's hard drinking inside the 'bedroom' of his house.*

Enter the **Chorus** *as strolling citizens of Wittenberg discussing the return of Faustus.*

Chorus 1	He's back, you know.
Chorus 2	I heard. They say he's travelled the world from Pole to Pole.
Chorus 4	Rescued Holy Bruno from the Pope's dungeons and flew him back to Germany on the back of a fury!
Chorus 3	*[Turning to audience confidingly]* Even the Emperor Charles is proud to number Faustus among his friends: this hero who rescued Germany's elected Pope; this genius who can conjure wonders on request!

Enter **Martino** *and* **Frederick,** *friends of* **Benvolio.**

Martino	… and they say Faustus means to conjure up the Emperor's entire family tree – show him his royal forebears and ancestors!
Frederick	… Apparently he can summon the most famous figures in all history: Dido, Queen of Carthage; Tamburlaine! Do let's go and see!

41

Martino	Where's Benvolio?
Frederick	Fast asleep, I'd lay odds. Last night he drank so much, that he must have a head like a stuffed owl on him this morning.

Benvolio pokes his head out of the 'window'.

Benvolio	*[Pained by the light]* Oh! Oh! What the devil's all the racket about?
Martino	Quiet, Benvolio, or the Devil might answer. We're off to the Emperor's Court. Haven't you heard? Doctor Faustus is back from Italy, with an army of one thousand fairies dancing attendance on him!
Benvolio	What of it?
Martino	Get yourself down here and come with us! They say there'll be magic no one's ever seen before!
Benvolio	Hasn't Bruno seen enough conjuring yet? I heard he rode home on the back of a hell-hound! If he's that much in love with the Devil let him elope to Rome with him, that's what I say.
Frederick	Are you coming down or not?
Benvolio	Not me. I'll watch from up here.
Martino	The Emperor is longing to see Faustus perform!
Benvolio	*[Slumping down, ill and sorry for himself]* I'm content to let my head hang out the window here and leave the rest of me in bed. Oh! There are demons doing the torments of Hell in my skull.

*Enter **Emperor Charles V**, the pregnant **Empress**, Bruno,
Faustus, **Wagner** and a crowd of admirers. Sound of cheering,
applause and cries of 'Faustus! Faustus!'. The three friends are
transfixed, though **Benvolio** registers only boredom and jaded
contempt. **Faustus** is sensitive to **Benvolio**'s asides and grows
increasingly irritated by him as the scene progresses.*

| Emperor | You have done our land a great service by fetching home Holy |

Bruno to the safety of my protection! The whole country thanks you, gentle Doctor Faustus.

Benvolio	*[Snide aside]* Not an Italian chef or Parma ham or anything useful!
Faustus	*[Bowing to the **Empress**]* Is there perhaps some service my arts can do the Empress, now I have returned? I know that ladies often crave the strangest things when a child is on the way.
Empress	Oh I would not dream –
Emperor	Cherries. She craves cherries! Ha! In the depth of winter, my lady craves the taste of summer! Even an Emperor cannot supply his lady with such tokens of love! What is a man to do?
Faustus	Allow me. I shall set my servant to the task immediately. *[Calling loudly offstage]* Mephistopheles! Cherries for her ladyship and with all speed!
Benvolio	How vilely this doctor tends to an aching skull!
Faustus	*[Aside]* I could do worse to your skull, believe me.
Emperor	But satisfy my curiosity: can you truly perform the wonders people talk of? Can you truly conjure the dead and fetch them from beyond the grave, for the living to see?
Faustus	Who would you care to see? Virgil or Xerxes? Nebuchadnezzar? Tamburlaine the Great? Or the pharaohs of ancient Egypt?
Benvolio	*[Aside]* Urgh! Anyone, for the love of God, so long as you do it *quietly*. I wouldn't go and see this charlatan in a theatre if they were giving away free tickets.
Emperor	Of all the world, I should like to see Alexander the Great – oh! – and his beautiful paramour,* of course.
Faustus	Then it will give me a world of pleasure to fetch them here.

*Enter **Mephistopheles** with a bowl of cherries, to gasps of astonishment. **Faustus** takes them and presents them to the **Empress**.*

* paramour – lover

Emperor	How is this possible? Cherries in winter?
Empress	And the sweetest I ever tasted, on my honour!
Faustus	As my studies have taught me, this round planet of ours, tilting and tumbling through the sun's rays, has seasons to north and south, as it has day and night to west and east. Its two hemispheres are threaded on the one axis, spinning around the frozen poles. When it's winter here, it's summer on the far side of the world. When our trees wear snow, the southern cherry trees are white with blossom. Somewhere on the earth it is always cherry season. For my servant, shod with magic, it is the work of a moment to travel there and back.
	He bows low to the **Empress**.
Benvolio	*[Aside]* This fourth-rate hoaxer – if I saw him at a summer fair, I'd pelt him with rotten apples! Would be better fun.
Faustus	*[Very loud]* Mephistopheles away! And with the solemn noise of trumpets, present before us mighty Alexander and the lovely Roxane!
Mephistopheles	Faustus, I will. *[Aside, to the audience]* Their likenesses, in any event. For is it not my sweet scholar's wish to use his magic to the *mightiest* ends?

Trumpets sound, repeatedly, at which **Benvolio**, *his hands over his ears, loses all patience.*

Benvolio Well? Where are they? If your spirits don't come soon, Doctor, I'll fall asleep with boredom. To think I wasted all this time standing gaping at a flimflam⋆ man, and there's not a thing to show for it! Huh!

Faustus *[Aside]* I'll give you something to show for it soon, if you don't hold your tongue. I beg you, Your Grace – when my spirits appear, do not speak to them, or go near. Simply watch in silence.

Emperor I won't forget, Faustus. I am content just to see the sight.

Benvolio *[Openly heckling now]* I'd be content, too, if there was anything worth watching around here. Calls himself a magician? He's no more a magician than I'm a reindeer. In faith, I've seen more reindeer taking Communion of a Sunday than I've seen magic around here today.

He puts his head down on his folded arms and pointedly goes to sleep.

Faustus *[Losing his temper, aside]* I'll give you reindeer, you buffoon.

He makes a horns hand-gesture towards **Benvolio**.

Trumpets sound again. While the audience's attention is diverted from him, **Benvolio** *'acquires' a pair of antlers larger than the window through which his head is sticking out. He is still asleep.*

Enter **Alexander the Great**, *right, and* **King Darius**, *left, wearing a golden crown. In a strong spotlight, they confront each other and fight in slow motion.* **Darius** *is killed. Enter the beautiful* **Roxane**, *right.*

Alexander takes off **Darius**'s *crown and sets it on* **Roxane**'s *head, then kisses her. Spellbound, the* **Emperor** *rises and goes towards the spirits.* **Alexander** *turns and appears to look at him. The* **Emperor** *goes to embrace* **Alexander**. **Faustus** *rushes to prevent them touching.*

Faustus Your Grace! Have a care! Remember what I said! These are spirits! Shadows! Likenesses …

⋆ flimflam – swindle someone with a confidence trick

Mephistopheles	*[To the audience]* Not, in fact, the real thing at all.
Faustus	*[To **Alexander, Darius** and **Roxane**]* Away! Be gone!
	***Alexander, Darius** and **Roxane** waft offstage. The **Emperor** looks downcast.*
Emperor	*[Sadly]* Your pardon, Faustus. The sight was so ravishing that I forgot myself … Are they gone, then? May I not –
	***Faustus**, to distract the **Emperor**, draws his attention to **Benvolio** in the window.*
Faustus	Look my gracious lord! Look at the strange beast in the window.
Emperor	Oh, marvellous!
	The crowd is hugely amused and roars with laughter and points.
Martino	Is he asleep or dead?
Wagner	Hey, Benvolio! Looks like the excitement has gone to your head!
Emperor	Well, something certainly has!
Wagner	*[Laughing]* Deer, deer, deer!
	***Benvolio** wakes up bad-temperedly and finds everyone staring up at him.*
Benvolio	What? What's everyone looking at? Oh, my head! Show over, is it? Good. I can get back to bed.
	He goes to pull his head back in through the window but fails, because of the spreading antlers. In his panic he cannot fit them backwards through the frame. He feels them with his hands, feels too the humiliation of being laughed at.
	Is this your doing, you … you … *scholar*?
Faustus	Oh surely not! How could it be, good sir? By your own account, Doctor Faustus is nothing but a flimflam man – no skill, no cunning, no magic art – in fact, a reindeer has more magic than this Doctor Faustus. I heard it said, just today! And so, my lord

Emperor, perhaps since I have achieved nothing more for you than to fetch cherries from the southern hemisphere and rescue Holy Bruno from imprisonment and produce visions of the mighty Alexander … let me make it up to you by raising up a kennel of hunting dogs and setting them on this … this … game young man. Come Belimore! Argiron! Asterote!

Benvolio *[Still struggling in the window, genuinely terrified]* No! Stop! Don't! He's raising up a pack of demons from Hell to tear me to pieces! Someone help me! I can't endure pain – can't stand pain! I've heard what the devil does to a damned man! I've seen the pictures on the church wall! Your mightiness – *please!*

Emperor Very well. Let me plead mercy for him. Set him loose, Doctor. He has done penance enough for his rudeness to you.

Faustus *[Bowing graciously, calm again]* My gracious lord, it wasn't done for my own satisfaction. It was simply to afford you and your lady a moment's harmless entertainment. I shall remove his horns straight away. Prune and pollard★ him, Mephistopheles … and Benvolio – mind you speak nothing but good of scholars, in future.

*At the foot of the ladder, **Mephistopheles** goes to remove the antlers.*

Benvolio *[Aside, descending the ladder]* Speak well of *you*? A man who pillories me in front of the Emperor – in front of the entire town? Scholars! *[He spits]* By God, I know what I'll study! I'll take a scholarship in Revenge. Tricks or no tricks, I'll kill you for this, Doctor.

Emperor Come Faustus! I'll find some way to recompense your genius! By my life, I will! You shall be my First Minister and rule the state of Germany!

Faustus Your Highness honours me greatly.

*Exit **Benvolio**, left. **Emperor** leads everyone else off right, the crowd marvelling. **Faustus**, laughing, hesitates at the edge of the stage, looking back at **Mephistopheles** who stands holding the antlers under his arm, centre stage.*

★ pollard – cut off the top and branches (of a tree)

Faustus	*[Trying to justify his petty act of spite]* A joke, that's all.
Mephistopheles	A moment's harmless entertainment. Quite.
Faustus	A joke.

Mephistopheles needs to say nothing.

I'm First Minister of Germany now, do you hear? I'll make her the glory of the world. A golden time for Germany and the Empire. Blazoned on the history books. Wisdom. Scholarship. Enlightenment …

Mephistopheles examines the antlers, frond by frond.

I'll do such things, Mephistopheles! Such great and wondrous things!

Mephistopheles	Sweet friend, why tell me? It goes without saying.

Exit Faustus.

[To the audience, curious] Did you see his terror? At the thought of a pack of demons coming to tear him limb from limb? He has seen the pictures on the church walls. The things demons do to a damned man. Did you see his terror?

He goes to leave, and then, to clarify, in case the audience has misunderstood him.

Benvolio, I mean. Benvolio. *[Laughs softly to himself]* A moment's harmless entertainment.

• •

SCENE 4

An isolated spot.

*Enter **Benvolio**, sword drawn, raging, closely followed by **Martino** and **Frederick** who are trying to pacify him.*

Benvolio	Please yourselves! It's all the same to me. See if I care. I'll do it alone. My head might weigh less without its antlers but my heart's molten lead inside me!

Martino	No, but listen, Benvolio! Let's talk about this at least!
Benvolio	You want me to just swallow it down? A trick like that? I'm a laughing stock! He made me a laughing stock! I'll kill him, I tell you! I'll kill that swindler! Shyster! Fraud! You want him to get off scot-free? What, when every groom, harlot, and boot boy in town points and sniggers at me in the street? May I never shut my eyes again till I've put my sword through that conjuror, Faustus. Are you with me or against me? This blade's going to peel the shame off me here and now, or I'd rather lay down and die on the spot!
Frederick	All right! All right! We'll help you – of course we will. Friends, no matter what.
	Benvolio hugs him.
Benvolio	Then help me set up the ambush just here. Faustus will be coming soon. I saw him kiss the Emperor's hand in farewell. He's laden down with presents and reward money. You can have my share of the money – so long as I have his blood.
	Frederick goes and keeps a look-out stage left.
Martino	Where shall I stand, Benvolio?
Benvolio	You and I shall wait till Frederick sets about him. Then we'll grab him from behind. Oh, if he'd just hurry up I'd lose the shame off my head quicker than I shed those antlers!
	Frederick, peeking offstage left, begins to signal wildly.
Frederick	Quiet! He's coming – and on his own, too! Get ready! Let's cut off his head!
Benvolio	*I'll* have that privilege!
	*Enter **Faustus** wearing an expensive cloak with the hood up. Frederick jumps out in front of him, bringing him to a halt. Benvolio approaches from behind, sword at the ready.*
	[To himself, under his breath] He's a dead man. Hell take his soul!
	*He drives his sword into **Faustus** who gives an incoherent cry.*

ACT 3 SCENE 4

DOCTOR FAUSTUS

Groan all you like, Doctor. I've come to put an end to your grievances once and for all!

*He strikes off **Faustus**'s head. The friends watch it roll across the stage. **Frederick** and **Martino** wander after it and stare down at the severed head. **Benvolio** stays by the body.*

The devil's dead!

Frederick	Was this the great Doctor Faustus who could summon demons from the halls of Hell and make the fallen angels tremble?
Martino	Was this the face that faked a thousand tricks?
Frederick	Was this the damned head that thought up how to shame our friend in front of the Emperor?
Benvolio	Yes, that's the head. And here's the body. *[He kicks it]* I'll hang it up like venison to cure. I'll nail antlers to that head of his and make a trophy for my window.

*In his triumph, he turns to face the audience, grinning, fists raised. Behind him **Faustus** gets up, leaving his cloak on the ground, intact and restored to life. He rests his chin on **Benvolio**'s shoulder as the others stare, incapable of speech.*

Martino	For God's sake, Frederick! Give him his head!
Faustus	Oh keep it, gentlemen. Keep it. I shall have heads enough to juggle with by the time I've finished with you three.
Benvolio	*[Desperate whisper, not daring to look round, but feeling Faustus's face with his hand]* The devil's alive again!
Faustus	*[Breaking away, walking up and down, and relishing the grisly words and their terror]* Don't you know anything, you botching crew of ignorant sots★? I was given twenty-four years of life on this earth. Guaranteed. You could have cut the flesh from my bones and chopped it up as fine as sand – my spirit would have returned to it one second later. You could have pulled out my guts yard by yard, minced my vital organs, drained me

★ sot – habitual drunkard

of blood and painted the walls of Wittenberg red – and within seconds I'd have been here again, breathing down your necks. You could have buried me under ten thousand tons of rock or drowned me under twenty thousand fathoms of ocean – I'd have been back amongst you before you could cry 'Mercy!' What? No more jokes? Isn't it funny any more? But why am I wasting *my* time educating you, when I could ask others to teach you a lesson. Asteroth! Belimoth! Mephistopheles!

*Enter **Mephistopheles**, **Asteroth** and **Belimoth**.*

Take these traitors on your backs and carry them up as high as Heaven –

Mephistopheles	As high as we are permitted to go.
Faustus	Then throw them down to deepest Hell.
Mephistopheles	*[To himself, shuddering]* 'Then throw them down'. Ah, I remember those words spoken by other lips. The day we angels fell.
Faustus	No, no, wait!
Mephistopheles	*[To himself, startled]* What? Forgiveness?
Faustus	First the world should see them suffer for their crimes. *[Slapping **Frederick** on the back]* Take this one, Belimoth, and throw him in some muddy bog deeper than his nostrils. *[Slapping **Martino** this time]* Take the other, Asteroth, and drag him through the woods – wherever the thorns are sharpest. *[With relish]* And you, my gentle Mephistopheles, find some rocky cliff to roll this Benvolio down – this one who had such plans for my body – and see to it that every bone in his body breaks.
Mephistopheles	*[Aside]* Not forgiveness, then.
Frederick	Have pity, Faustus! Spare our lives, in God's sweet name!
Faustus	Take them away.

The three devils flinch from the name of God, but then start dragging the three ambushers off.

Frederick	They say a man must go where the devil drives.

*Exit **Mephistopheles, Asteroth, Belimoth, Frederick, Benvolio** and **Martino.***

Faustus	Come my trusty bodyguard, and escort me home! *[To audience]* These woods could teem with monsters, bears and cut-throats, but am I worried? A man with fifty thousand demon troopers at his command has precious little to fear, wouldn't you say?

*He clicks his fingers above his head. The sound of snare drums and marching feet builds to a deafening crescendo while **Faustus** picks up his cloak and swaggeringly puts it on. He goes over for a last look at the severed head. Close-up, it makes more of an impact on him. He touches it, then covers his mouth as if he is going to be sick.*

*Enter **Mephistopheles** left. With one small hand gesture he silences the drumming, so that **Faustus** looks round in surprise. Then **Faustus** recovers his arrogant composure.*

And when you're done, trot all three through town with a pair of … you know … on their heads. You know …

He mimes antlers with his hands but cannot call the right word to mind.

Those great … things.

Mephistopheles	Ah yes. Those great things, Faustus. Those 'great and wondrous things' you were set to achieve. I understand you perfectly. Strange. Don't they seem to you somehow … reduced?

***Faustus** is reminded of his grand plans in comparison with the pettiness of what has just happened.*

Faustus	What, that? That was just … an interlude. A piece of comic relief …

*The sound of **Frederick, Martino** and **Benvolio** screaming and begging for mercy.*

They interrupted the truly … That had nothing to do with … Now I can get back to …

Mephistopheles	To doing great and wondrous things. Yes.
	A church bell starts to strike, like a clock marking off the hours.
	Best be quick, though, Faustus. Time is moving on.
	Faustus, trying not to listen, kicks the dummy head offstage. Then his hand flies to his head, his guts, the wrist where he drew blood to use as ink.
	[Tenderly] The years are gathering behind you, sweet friend.
	Exit Faustus looking purposeful.
	[Less tenderly, to the audience] Like wolves behind a stag.

ACT 4

• •

SCENE 1

	*In front of drawn curtains, **Faustus**'s study behind. A jug of wine stands front stage right. Behind the curtain is a table heaped with food, a carving knife and some glasses. Behind the table is a bench where **Faustus**, **Mephistopheles** and various scholars are sitting.*
	*Enter **Faustus**'s servant, **Wagner**, right, having a laughing fit. He pauses for breath, hands on knees. He is much older than the last time we saw him.*
Wagner	*[To audience, indicating something that has just happened offstage right.]* Oh, that was funny! You should have seen! There was this horse dealer. You know Faustus's horse, eh? The one he conjured? Wondrous beast! Magnificent piece of horseflesh! Smooth as Satan! Could gallop fifty miles in an hour and never break sweat. Well, this horse dealer sees the horse and wants to buy it. Offers him a putrid ten florins. 'Deal!' says the Master. 'Just don't take it anywhere near water.' Well, you know how people are once you tell them not to do a thing. Off

he goes to the river, this horse dealer, quick as a dog down a rabbit hole. Tries to cross the river. And the horse – *[Miming]* it just up and melts between his legs! Melts! Like butter on a roasting spit! He comes raging back, this horse dealer, demanding his money back. And then his wife! Then his neighbour, then his brother-in-law. All demanding a refund! Least, they do till the Doctor magics the noise out of them! *[Mimes people struck dumb and still complaining, missing their voices, grasping their throats]* Off they go, all gaping like goldfish. Laugh? I thought I'd –

He breaks off, suddenly sobered, then tries to carry on. From behind the curtain comes the occasional burst of raucous laughter: a party.

He's a rare one, the Doctor, with his pranks and jokes. People with antlers on their heads … Making monkeys of his enemies. Making them look … People say he's a genius. Cleverest man in the whole University. Cleverest man in Wittenberg. Cleverest man in the *universe*! *[Shrugs, points to his head]* But that's in here. No telling from outside, is there? How would I know, someone like me? I can't see inside people's heads. I like the jokes! That horse dealer! Ha! Laugh? I could've –

*Noise of a drinking glass breaking. Suddenly **Wagner** is entirely serious, ashen, disturbed, confused.*

I think my master means to die soon. He made his will yesterday. *[Trying to be delighted but failing]* Left me all his money! And his house! Everything in it. Gold plate. Two thousand gold ducats. But if he's ill … Never! Hasn't aged a day. Not since the magic started. Twenty years back. More! *[Pauses to calculate on his fingers]* Twenty-three years back. Is it really that long? But there's him still young and fit and always rushing about … Makes me tired just to watch him. Rushing here. Rushing there. Like there's a dog at the seat of his pants. 'Time's wasting, Wagner! Time's wasting!' Hear him say it time after …

Ashen again, he repeats himself.

I think my master means to die soon. He made his will yesterday.

*The curtain draws to reveal **Faustus**, **Mephistopheles** and three students, sitting along the far side of a table (like Leonardo's 'Last Supper'), all in cheerful mood. The **students** have their heads together trying to decide who was the most beautiful woman ever to have lived. **Wagner** picks up the jug of wine, goes to them and refills their glasses, still talking to the audience.*

But if he thought Death was close, he wouldn't be swilling and revelling like this with his students, would he? This feast tonight – food and wine enough for an army!

Wagner collects some dirty dishes and goes off.

First student	All right! We are agreed! The most beautiful woman who ever lived? Helen of Troy! That's what the legend says. Prince Paris won from the gods 'the love of the most beautiful woman in the world'. And anyway, she must have been, to start a ten-year war between the world's greatest heroes!
Mephistopheles	*[Aside]* Beautiful. Or lovable. Or an excuse to shed blood.
First student	Helen of Troy!
Second student	So will you, Doctor? Would you? Can you … by your arts, I mean … let us see her?
Third student	The most beautiful woman who ever lived? We'd be forever grateful!
Faustus	I know, I know. It is not my way to refuse my friends any wish it's in my power to grant. You shall see her, as she was the day Prince Paris eloped with her and set sail over the sea to Troy!

They start to celebrate noisily.

But you must be quiet. Keep silent. While the magic is working, there is a danger in words.

Mephistopheles	*[Raising a glass to **Faustus**]* Oh, there is always a danger in words, Faustus.
Faustus	Mephistopheles! Bring forth the fair Helen, whose beauty struck sparks from ten thousand swords and spilled blood from as many battle wounds!

*Mephistopheles claps his hands and music sounds. He goes off and ushers in **Helen of Troy**, head covered by a veil. He stands her facing them (back to the audience) and lifts off her veil. Amused and a little drunk, **Faustus** watches the students' delight, then glances at **Helen** and is transfixed by her beauty. **Mephistopheles** covers her again and leads her offstage. The music fades.*

First student   She was … *[Trails off]*

Second student   There aren't words.

Third student   The finest creation of Nature.

First student   If I live to be a hundred I'll never …

Third student   Blessings on you, Doctor, for showing us this sight.

Second student   *[Shaking himself back to the present and getting up]* Yes, yes. All agreed on that! May you be blessed with everlasting happiness for the pleasure you've given us this evening!

*A clock strikes. **Faustus** jumps and spills his wine over his lap. He and **Mephistopheles** look at one another. Attentively, **Mephistopheles** hurries to mop him up.*

Mephistopheles   *[Tenderly and low]* Well, not 'everlasting', perhaps.

Faustus   *[To the students]* And the same to you, gentlemen. I wish the same to you. Farewell.

*Exit the **students**, still talking about **Helen of Troy**. He calls after them, not liking his own company.*

Farewell. Come again when you have the time! Come again. … If I have the time … Mephistopheles, that vision – it filled me with such a craving …

Mephistopheles   Shall I fetch her again?

*He makes to exit left but halts when an **Old man** enters right and begins to reason and plead with **Faustus**. **Mephistopheles** watches from a distance, not attempting to intervene.*

Old man   Doctor Faustus! Doctor Faustus! Oh, my dear young man!

	Give up this cursed magic of yours! It will damn your soul to Hell. It will rob you of salvation!
Faustus	Who are you? How did you get in?
Old man	So far you have only sinned like a man – strayed from God's commandments. That's human! But don't persist in it like a devil! You are a good man, a kind man! But if sin becomes a habit – a way of life – you'll leave it too late to see your error and repent! Think of it – banished from Heaven for ever! Damned to everlasting Hell. Torments past description. Torments past human imagination!
Faustus	Leave me alone, old man!
Old man	I know my words sound harsh, but I only say them out of love. Love for the goodness in you. Pity for what might become of you. If I could block your path to destruction, halt this downward slide towards Hell …!
Faustus	*Stop!*

*The action freezes. **Faustus** stands bolt upright drenched in spotlight.*

What have I done? Damned? Damned, Faustus! *Damned!* My time is almost gone! The end is nearly here! Wretch that I am! I can hear Hell calling; summoning me! No hope … despair! There's no hope for me. None at all. Nothing but despair, tearing into me like grappling irons! All right! All right! I'm coming, Lucifer! Why go on, fearing it, watching it coming closer and closer and closer and closer and closer and clo– I should finish it here and now. Pay Hell its due. Stop pretending … stop deluding myself.

*He searches around for something. **Mephistopheles** comes back to the front of the table, picks up a carving knife and moves to circle the table. Enter an **angel**, who places himself between **Mephistopheles** and **Faustus**. Without much effort, **Mephistopheles** wins the battle of wills and moves the **angel** aside. Then he presents the knife to **Faustus** with a bow. **Mephistopheles** returns to his previous position at the side of the* *stage.* **Faustus** *opens his collar and goes to stab himself. The spotlight goes out.*

Old man

Stop, Faustus! Don't do it! Don't give in to the sin of despair! Despair – the only unforgivable sin! Look! I see an angel hovering over your head with a vial of precious grace ready to pour into your soul! Call on God's mercy! It is yours for the asking!

Faustus

*[To the **Old man**, as he sets down the knife]* Oh my dear friend … you offer such comfort to a soul in torment. Leave me a while. I have to think. I have to examine my poor, dark soul.

Old man

I will go. But my heart aches for you, son. I fear for that unhappy soul of yours.

*Exit **Old man**. **Mephistopheles** steps into his path and they look into each others' eyes, but the **Old man** simply steps round **Mephistopheles**, unfazed.*

***Faustus** sits down again, head in hands, at the end of the table. **Mephistopheles** moves round behind him, seemingly attentive and reassuring, hands poised over his head as if about to stroke his hair.*

Faustus

Faustus, you cursed wretch, what have you done? I repent my sins. I do! I repent the sin of despair … and yet I'm still drowning in it! Drowning in despair …

He clutches his chest as if suffering a heart attack.

The devils and angels are fighting for the upper hand in here! Hell and Heaven are at war inside my chest! Think, Faustus! What to do to get out of this snare – to win back the bliss you threw away.

*Suddenly **Mephistopheles** loops the knotted cord of his friar's belt round **Faustus**'s throat and begins to strangle him. **Faustus** screams and tries to pull free, but cannot. He is thrown off his seat and onto his knees at **Mephistopheles**'s feet.*

Mephistopheles

Traitor, Faustus! I arrest your soul for breach of contract, for the breaking of your solemn bond, for disobedience to my sovereign lord, Lucifer! Recant*, or I'll tear you to pieces.

Faustus I'm sorry! I'm sorry! I repent! I repent! *I repent!* Forgive me, Mephistopheles! *Sweet* Mephistopheles!

Mephistopheles lets him go just as suddenly and refastens his belt. Faustus kneels at his feet, sobbing, clutching his robe, begging forgiveness.

I'm sorry! Forgive me! Speak to your master for me! Beg him to forgive me! I'm sorry if I gave offence! I'm sorry I went back on my word! But let me live! Just a little while longer … Let me live!

Faustus rolls up his sleeve and takes the carving knife off the table.

Look, look! I'll sign the contract all over again! I will! I'll renew my vow to Lucifer!

Mephistopheles Do it, Faustus, before Lucifer hears about this. When he does, he will mark you down for the worst torments Hell offers.

Clumsily Faustus stabs himself in the arm again, turning away from the audience to achieve this. The whole stage is swamped in red light. The words appear, letter by letter, projected on the back wall: I Faustus …

Faustus crouches at Mephistopheles's feet, the devil stroking his hair now, soothingly.

Faustus It was that old man's fault – trying to tempt me away from Lucifer, frightening me with talk of Hell and torment. Stupid, canting fool of a cripple! It's him should be tormented! *[Becoming sadistic and loud]* Torment him, why don't you, sweet Mephistopheles, with the worst Hell can do!

Mephistopheles *[Quietly factual]* His faith is very strong. His soul's beyond my reach … But I'll do what I can to his body – whatever old age hasn't already done. *[Tipping Faustus's face up towards his]* And what other service can I do my sweet Faustus while I'm gone?

* recant – say that one no longer holds an opinion or belief

Faustus	There is something that would satisfy all my heart's desires.
Mephistopheles	And you haven't mentioned it before?
Faustus	If I could only have Helen! When you showed us earlier … I never saw … If I could only have Helen of Troy for my lover … in her arms I could forget everything – everything that tempts me to disobey!
Mephistopheles	You shall have her, in the twinkling of an eye.

*Mephistopheles goes offstage and fetches **Helen of Troy**, as before. Again, **Mephistopheles** lifts up her veil to reveal her face. **Faustus** is enraptured.*

Faustus	Is this the face that launched a thousand ships, and set on fire the lofty towers of Troy?

She extends a hand to him. Mesmerized, he rises and goes to her.

Sweet Helen, make me immortal with a kiss.

They kiss.

Her lips unsettle my soul, like a bird from its tree! Look where it flies! Oh Helen, give me back my soul!

They kiss again.

Here's where I'll stay, for Heaven is in your lips, and everything is dross that isn't you. *[Becoming more and more excitedly, expansively happy]* I'll be your Prince Paris: rivals for your love can burn down Wittenberg in their longing to have you home! And I'll do combat with feeble Menelaus and wear your colours in my helmet's plumes – and wound Achilles in his Achilles' heel and hurry back to Helen for a kiss. Oh! You are lovelier than the evening's air, clad in the beauty of a thousand stars! You are Zeus when he appeared to Semele and scorched her to nothingness with the sheer brilliance of his glory! You are sunny Apollo swimming in the watery arms of Arethusa, his river lover. No one but you. No one but you, Helen! I'll have no one but you for my lover! You are all I'll ever need!

They kiss again.

Mephistopheles [*To the audience, producing from his pocket the materials he has used to fabricate the likeness of **Helen of Troy***] A rag. A bone. A hank of hair. She was a moment in the making. A likeness, remember.

*When the **Old man** re-enters right, **Faustus** is so absorbed in **Helen** that he does not even look round.*

Old man Cursed Faustus! Wicked man. You've slammed the Gates of Heaven against yourself! You've barred yourself from the holy courts of God's Justice!

*Two **devils** enter left, heavily armed with instruments of torture – blades, whips, hooks. They move towards the **Old man** menacingly, threateningly.*

My own test of faith is here, I see. The furnace gapes for me, where God tempers our mettle★. But my faith will triumph over you, vile Lucifer! Do your petty worst, you fiends. Soon my God will snatch me high up out of your reach!

*The **devils** drag him offstage left and he can be heard screaming. **Helen of Troy**, in kissing **Faustus**, covers his ears. They exit together.*

● ●

SCENE 2

*Faustus's study. Two grand chairs are set in front of the audience, facing the stage, rendering the audience among the demon hosts of **Lucifer**.*

*Enter **Lucifer** and **Beelzebub**, both carrying staffs. Enter **Mephistopheles** behind them. **Beelzebub** and **Lucifer** seat themselves in the chairs.*

*Mephistopheles's feelings, whether of pity or contempt for **Faustus**, should remain unclear.*

Beelzebub We shall watch it from here.

Lucifer The end. The final scene. It will happen here, in this room.

★ mettle – a person's ability to cope well with difficulties

61

Beelzebub	The expiry of the contract. The forfeit of Faustus's soul.
Lucifer	We shall sit here and watch how he conducts himself in the face of damnation.
Mephistopheles	*[To audience]* How will he? Already, terror has dried up his heart's blood. His brain teems with schemes to outwit the Devil and slip through the net. But he knows it can't be done. The pleasures he ate were spiced with poison. He has dined on his own destruction.
	Faustus and Wagner enter, Wagner happy, Faustus red-eyed, white-faced and nervous.
Faustus	Well, Wagner? How do you like the terms of my will?
Wagner	Wonderful well, master! Marvellous well! You won't be sorry! I'll be your good and faithful servant all my days, sir, so help me I will!
	*Enter the three **students**.*
Faustus	Thank you, Wagner. Welcome, gentlemen.
First student	Doctor! Your honour! Oh, but you look so … changed.
Faustus	Oh gentlemen!
Second student	Whatever's the matter, sir?
Faustus	Oh my friend … We shared a room at the University, did we not? If only I was still there, I might have gone on living. Now I must die. Everlastingly. *[Pause]* Listen! Is that Him? Is He coming?
First student	My dear Faustus! What are you so afraid of?
Second student	Just last week we were all so jolly together! And now …
Third student	*[To the other **students**]* He's been spending too much time alone. That's what it is.
Second student	We'll call a physician, then. You'll be well again in no time, sir!
Third student	Something you've eaten …
Faustus	A diet of sin, yes, which has damned me, body and soul.

Second student	Oh, if it's your conscience that's troubling you, remember – God's mercy is infinite! A man's conscience can be washed clean in the blood of –
Faustus	But my sin can never be pardoned! The snake that tempted Eve in the Garden of Eden will be forgiven before damnable Faustus. Listen! There's no time! Listen, gentlemen: don't be afraid; the danger's not yours. Listen! How long have I been a student here at the University? Thirty years? Believe me, as Hell's my witness, I wish I'd never seen Wittenberg; wish I'd never read a book; died ignorant. I've worked some wonders, haven't I? I've served Germany a little, haven't I? I've served the world of learning? It's cost me everything; cost me the world – Heaven, too, God knows! Heaven and God's sweet love. The kingdom of joy … *[Truly pitiful]* Instead, I'm bound for Hell. *[Pause]* Hell. Hell for ever. Oh, my sweet friends. What will become of Faustus, being in Hell for ever?
Second student	Call on God, then, Faustus!
Faustus	The God I forswore★, you mean? The God I cursed and blasphemed★★?
	*The **students** draw back, leaving **Faustus** isolated. **Lucifer** and **Beelzebub** point their staffs at **Faustus**, exerting irresistible forces on his body.*
	Oh, my God, I would weep, but the devil has drunk all my tears. I ought to weep blood – my life – my soul! Anything, but I should weep! Oh, my tongue! He stiffens my tongue to silence me!
Wagner	Who, master?
Faustus	I would lift up my hands to Heaven, but see, they're holding them … They're holding them!
Students (all)	Who, Faustus?
Faustus	Can't you see? Lucifer and Beelzebub! I gave them my soul in exchange for knowledge.

★ forswore – agreed to give up or do without
★★ blasphemed – spoke disrespectfully about God or sacred things

| First student | God forbid! |

Faustus *[Laughing stridently]* Oh God did! Oh yes! God forbade it, but Faustus did it anyway! For the luxury of twenty-four little years, the good doctor paid the price: all hope of eternal joy! *[He bows]* I wrote out a contract in my own blood. The contract expires tonight. This is the time, and he will fetch me.

First student Why didn't you tell us this before? Priests could have prayed for you!

Faustus They threatened to tear me to pieces if I named God; to haul me down to Hell if I paid any heed of religion. Now it is too late. Go, gentlemen. If you stay, you may die along with me.

Second student Tell us what to do, Faustus! What can we do to save you?

Faustus Forget me. Save yourselves. Go.

Third student I'll stay with you! God will shield me!

First student *[Recognizing a lost cause]* Do not tempt God, friend. Let's go into the next room and pray for him there.

Faustus Yes. Pray for me. Pray for me … But whatever noise you hear, don't come in. Nothing and no one can save me now.

Second student Pray, Faustus! And we will too, that God takes mercy on you.

Faustus *[Shaking hands with them]* Goodbye, gentlemen. If I live till morning, I'll come and find you. Otherwise … Faustus has gone to Hell.

*The **students** leave, right. As **Faustus** shuts the door behind them, **Mephistopheles** mounts the stage, left.*

Mephistopheles Yes, Faustus. Now all hope is gone. Turn your thoughts to Hell. That's where you'll make your bed tonight.

Faustus *[Starting to cry]* Treacherous fiend! It was you who tempted me, wasn't it? It's you who've robbed me of eternal happiness!

Mephistopheles *[Gently, tenderly]* I confess it, Faustus. It was my doing. Whenever you strayed away from me, towards Heaven, I blocked your path. Whenever you picked up a Bible, my breath fluttered the pages. Anything to keep you by me. What, are you crying? A little late for that, isn't it? Until midnight. Then we shall be together. Always.

*Exit **Mephistopheles**, left. A huge clock face is projected against the backdrop, its hands at ten o'clock and moving. The ticking of the clock gets louder and louder until it is deafening. **Faustus** is driven to his knees, covering his ears as he tries to shut out the sound. It stops, as **Good Angel** and **Bad Angel** enter from opposite sides of the stage. **Good Angel** is holding a golden crown which is suspended by wires.*

Good Angel Oh Faustus, if only you had listened! Countless joys would have roosted in your heart. But you loved life more than your soul.

Bad Angel *[With relish]* Now you must endure Hell's pains for evermore.

Good Angel What good will your money and power do you now? Your influence and party tricks and fleshly delights?

Bad Angel More things to miss when you lie naked and bereft of everything, in Hell.

*Now in agreement, the two **angels** find themselves standing in identical postures on either side of the stage, and look each other*

65

*over. They move towards each other, as if they might shake hands; even converse. **Good Angel** raises a hand to bless the **Bad Angel**. **Bad Angel** flinches and makes the 'horns' hand gesture in a curse. They are enemies again. **Good Angel** moves behind the kneeling **Faustus** and holds the golden crown over his head. A spotlight pours down on him and the crown.*

Good Angel   See what glory was waiting for you if you had chosen the straight and narrow way? Celestial happiness! Unspeakable joy! Bliss without end! This crown to wear, and a throne at the right hand of God! Look up and see the bright and shining saints as they share in the timeless triumph of good!

Faustus looks up into the light and reaches for the crown which then floats upwards beyond reach.

But now, poor soul, I make my farewell.
For see: the gates are opening to Hell.

*Smoke and the noise of roaring fire booms out from offstage left. Exit **Good Angel**, right. Horrified, **Faustus** gazes offstage into the fire, hands in his hair.*

Bad Angel   Yes, Faustus, feast your eyes on that instead. Our vast and splendid torture house, stoked with the souls of the Damned. See how they are tossed on burning forks and plunged in molten lead? See where the idle rest their weary bones in white-hot chairs; throw themselves down to sleep on burning coals, dreaming of death but never able to die? See how the truth is dragged out with hooks through the mouths of liars; how misers are locked in treasure chests full of scorpions, to count their fortunes in stings. Gluttons who left the poor to starve feed perpetually now on drops of fire. Lechers who burned with lust in life, burn for it like spit-roast pork, wishing they had been born like the angels: genderless. The pitiless plead with the whip for pity. Murderers hunt Hell for someone to help them die …

Faustus   I've seen enough! The sight is torture enough!

Bad Angel   [*Mocking*] But you are Faustus – famed in Earth and Hell! The most indulged, greatest, most damnable doctor of Wittenberg; worst sinner of them all! Those who climb highest have the furthest to fall. Till midnight, Faustus.

*Exit **Bad Angel**, left. The smoke and noise stop. The ticking grows louder, then a clock strikes eleven.*

Faustus One hour! A bare one hour to live! And then … an endless torment of unendurable pain! *No!*

Panicked, he opens one after another of the books hanging from their chains, trying to find spells to save himself. Instead, ash spills out of each book.

You planets spinning through the frozen wastes of space – stand still! Stop, Time, so midnight never comes! Send me back the sun! Let the sun rise again and shine for ever and ever and keep off the dark! Or let this one hour last a year, a month, a week, one single *day*, and give me time to repent! The seconds are trampling me down; the minutes are stampeding over me! The black horses of night are dragging me down to Hell! Someone stop them – the black horses! *[To audience] Please!*

There is a long pause during which we hear the sound of the clock ticking grow from soft to loud again.

The stars go on moving. Time goes on passing. The clock will strike. The devil will come. And Faustus will be damned. *[A new thought, a false hope]* I'll leap up to my God!

Lucifer *and **Beelzebub** point their staffs and **Faustus**'s upraised arms are 'pulled' down and he is hurled to the ground.*

But I can't! Who's pulling me down?

Suddenly the stage is swamped in blood-red light.

See where Christ's blood streams across the sky! One drop would save my soul. Half a drop! Oh, my Christ!

He clutches his chest in terrible pain.

No! Don't tear out my heart for naming Christ! I will call on him! I will! Oh spare me, Lucifer.

*At the mention of **Lucifer**, the red light goes out.*

No! Gone.

*Looking directly upwards, **Faustus** sees the face of God in judgement.*

I see you, Lord! Oh Lord, my God, No! I fear that frown worse than Lucifer's! I fear that damning finger! Mountains and hills fall on me and hide me from the wrath of God! *No!* *[Clawing at the floor]* Open, won't you? Open and let me hide! It won't open! The Earth won't swallow me! *[Climbing on to the table to reach higher]* You stars! You constellations! You fixed my fate, didn't you, the day I was born? You wrote my horoscope on the cosmos! You allotted me this cursed life! So? Help me! Draw me up like a foggy mist into the bowels of that thundercloud. Spew out my limbs – my bones, my flesh – but let my soul rise up to Heaven! My soul at least!

The clock is once more projected on the backdrop reading half past eleven. It is replaced by an hourglass almost running out.

Half an hour gone! Soon the rest. Soon it will all be gone. Oh God, if you won't spare my soul, at least set some limit on my pain! Let Faustus live in Hell a thousand years … a hundred thousand, but at the end be saved! Nothing lasts for ever! Everything comes to an end! Except the torments of the damned. Why wasn't I born without a soul? Why not an animal that lives and dies and rots and turns to dust? Or why can't my soul be mortal too? Why can't the old religions have been right that said our souls fly out of us and into doves and bears and fish and *[Crouching as if to study a beetle or ant]* tiny, witless, worthless, brainless … *[He stamps on the beetle]* All beasts are happy; their souls dissolve away into the elements. But mine must go on living, to be crushed in Hell. *[To audience]* Curse you. Curse the parents who brought me into the world and left me alone to find my way out of it … *[Repenting at last]* No, Faustus. Curse yourself. Curse Lucifer who deprived you of Heaven.

The clock starts to strike twelve. Thunder and lightning.

It strikes. Now body, turn to air, or Lucifer will send you straight to Hell. Oh soul, be changed into little water drops and fall into the ocean, never to be found.

Lucifer and Beelzebub mount the stage, left; Mephistopheles, right. Devils enter through the door in the backdrop armed with implements of torture. Smoke and roaring fire issue again from 'Hell'.

My God, *my God … look not so fierce on me!* Ugly Hell, don't gape. Spare me, Lucifer! Let me go. *[Shouting upwards]* I'll burn my books!

He turns to run from Lucifer and Beelzebub but is confronted by Mephistopheles, to whom he appeals for help.

Ah Mephistopheles!

Mephistopheles makes an impulsive gesture of love, reaching out his arms, hands hidden by the sleeves of his habit. Faustus runs into his embrace and they look into each other's faces. Then Mephistopheles shakes back his cuffs to reveal a meat-hook in each hand, sinks them into Faustus's back, and drags him away to Hell, left.

• •

SCENE 3

Faustus's empty study. The chains hang empty from the ceiling. The table has collapsed. Items of Faustus's clothing (e.g. a boot, a belt) lie strewn on the floor. Also the 'head' used in Act 2, scene 4.

Enter the three students nervously.

First student	Those ghastly noises!
Second student	Those terrible screams!
Third student	The fire storm that swept the house! I pray God it wasn't … the blood, the stench! These rags – what are they?
Second student	Sweet God. What happened in here?
First student	Nothing that started in this world.

69

He goes over to investigate the 'head' and covers his mouth and gags in horror and nauseous disgust.

Oh help us, Heaven! They tore the poor ... they tore him limb from limb!

Third student   They turned on him at last, then. Those demons of his.

Second student   He was such a scholar. Such a great mind! He taught us students such things. Everyone said how wise he was, the marvellous Doctor Faustus! All he wanted was to know; to understand. Is that such a sin?

His colleagues hush him, one putting a hand over his mouth to silence the blasphemy.

First student   We'll give him a Christian burial ... what parts we can find ...

*Exit **First student**.*

Third student   I'll wear mourning, for one.

*Exit **Third student**.*

Second student   *[To audience, bitterly]* Cut is the branch that might have grown straight.
Burned are the scholar's works.
Faustus is gone, so learn from his fate,

If in you too there lurks
The longing to question and wonder at things
God would sooner withhold.
For the brightness of intellect may singe
Your name from the Book of Gold.

*Exit **Second student**. Curtain down.*

Image from the title page of an early printing of *Doctor Faustus*.

Activities

Year 7

KEY STAGE 3 FRAMEWORK OBJECTIVES	RELEVANT ACTIVITIES CHAPTER(S)
Word Level	
12 Using a dictionary	Choices and consequences
13 Spellcheckers	Writing a persuasive letter
14 Word meaning in context	Morality plays; Faustus on trial; A new comic scene
15 Dictionary and thesaurus	Morality plays; Writing a persuasive letter
21 Subject vocabulary	Choices and consequences
Sentence Level	
8 Starting paragraphs	Writing a persuasive letter
9 Main point of paragraph	Writing a persuasive letter
11 Sentence variety	Writing a persuasive letter
12 Sequencing paragraphs	Writing a persuasive letter
13 e) Persuasion	Writing a persuasive letter
15 Vary formality	Choices and consequences
17 Standard English	Choices and consequences
Reading	
1 Locate information	Morality plays; A new comic scene; A dramatic ending
2 Extract information	Choices and consequences; Morality plays; A new comic scene; A dramatic ending
4 Note-making	Morality plays; A dramatic ending
6 Active reading	A new comic scene
7 Identify main ideas	Choices and consequences; A new comic scene; A dramatic ending
8 Infer and deduce	Morality plays; A new comic scene
9 Distinguish writer's views	A new comic scene
12 Character, setting and mood	A new comic scene
15 Endings	A dramatic ending
18 Response to a play	Morality plays
20 Literary heritage	Morality plays
Writing	
1 Drafting process	Writing a persuasive letter; Inventing a moral tale
2 Planning formats	Writing a persuasive letter, Inventing a moral tale
3 Exploratory writing	Inventing a moral tale
4 Handwriting and presentation	Writing a persuasive letter
5 Story structure	Inventing a moral tale
6 Characterization	A new comic scene; Inventing a moral tale
10 Organize texts appropriately	Choices and consequences
11 Present information	Choices and consequences
15 Express a view	Writing a persuasive letter

Speaking and Listening

1	Clarify through talk	Choices and consequences; Morality plays; Faustus on trial; A new comic scene; Inventing a moral tale; A dramatic ending
5	Put a point of view	Morality plays; Faustus on trial
6	Recall main points	Faustus on trial
7	Pertinent questions	Faustus on trial
10	Report main points	Morality plays; Faustus on trial
11	Range of roles	Morality plays; Faustus on trial
12	Exploratory talk	Morality plays; Faustus on trial; Inventing a moral tale; A dramatic ending
13	Collaboration	Morality plays; Faustus on trial; Inventing a moral tale; A dramatic ending
14	Modify views	Morality plays; Faustus on trial; Inventing a moral tale; A dramatic ending
15	Explore in role	Faustus on trial; A new comic scene; Inventing a moral tale
16	Collaborate on scripts	A new comic scene; Inventing a moral tale
18	Exploratory drama	A new comic scene
19	Evaluate presentations	A new comic scene; Inventing a moral tale

Year 8

KEY STAGE 3 FRAMEWORK OBJECTIVES	RELEVANT ACTIVITIES CHAPTER(S)
Word Level	
6 Dictionaries and spellcheckers	Choices and consequences
6c) Dictionaries and spellcheckers	Writing a persuasive letter
9 Specialist vocabulary	Choices and consequences; Morality plays
12 Formality and word choice	Choices and consequences; Writing a persuasive letter
Sentence Level	
2 Variety of sentence structure	Writing a persuasive letter
6 Grouping sentences	Writing a persuasive letter
7 Cohesion and coherence	Writing a persuasive letter
12 Degrees of formality	Choices and consequences; Writing a persuasive letter
Reading	
3 Note-making formats	Morality plays; A dramatic ending
5 Trace developments of themes	Choices and consequences; Morality plays; A new comic scene; A dramatic ending
7 Implied and explicit meanings	Morality plays; A new comic scene
10 Development of key ideas	Choices and consequences; Morality plays; A dramatic ending
14 Literary conventions	Morality plays
15 Historical context	Morality plays
16 Cultural context	Morality plays
Writing	
1 Effective planning	Writing a persuasive letter; Inventing a moral tale
2 Anticipate reader reaction	Choices and consequences; Writing a persuasive letter; Inventing a moral tale
3 Writing to reflect	A new comic scene; Inventing a moral tale
5 Narrative commentary	A new comic scene; Inventing a moral tale
7 Establish the tone	A new comic scene; Writing a persuasive letter
8 Experiment with conventions	A new comic scene
12 Formal description	Choices and consequences
13 Present a case persuasively	Writing a persuasive letter
14 Develop an argument	Writing a persuasive letter
16 Balanced analysis	Choices and consequences
17 Integrate evidence	Choices and consequences
Speaking and Listening	
3 Formal presentation	Faustus on trial
5 Questions to clarify or refine	Morality plays; Faustus on trial
6 Evaluate own listening	Faustus on trial
7 Listen for a specific focus	Faustus on trial
9 Evaluate own contributions	A new comic scene; Inventing a moral tale

Choices and consequences

One of the main themes of Doctor Faustus is making decisions. Throughout the play, Doctor Faustus has to make decisions, but he also has to take the consequences of those choices. In the opening scene we see Faustus in his study. He is at a 'crossroads' in his life. He is a respected doctor at the University of Wittenberg in Germany, but needs to decide what subject he will study further. He considers:

- Philosophy
- Law
- Medicine
- Theology.

1   With a partner, discuss what you know about these subjects. Use a dictionary to check your understanding of them.

2   Here are the reasons Faustus gives for rejecting these subjects, but in a random order.

- It discourages people from thinking freely.
- There is little point in this because everyone dies anyway.
- It is just arguing on behalf of other people.
- It is just a way of winning every argument.

Match each subject with the reason that Faustus rejects it. Choose relevant quotations from the play to back up your choices. Write your answers like this:

Doctor Faustus decides not to study ... because he believes ... He says '...'.

Magic

The subject that Faustus *does* decide to study is magic. It is not the kind of magic that entertains people at parties, such as card tricks and producing rabbits from hats, but the more sinister black magic. Black magic involves the supposed calling up of evil and dead spirits (necromancy) in order to foretell the future. It also involves gaining excessive power by invoking evil forces, to change the natural order of things. Faustus believes that magic will make him 'Emperor of the world'.

1   Scan Act 1, Scene 1 to find out exactly what Faustus, Valdes and Cornelius think magic will give them or enable them to do.
2   Now look at Act 2, Scene 1. Describe, in your own words, three of the places that Faustus travelled to.
3   Where was he unable to go and why?

The bargain

With his magic powers, Faustus summons Mephistopheles. Through him, Faustus makes a bargain with Lucifer, the Devil, which is sealed with the signing of a deed (document).

1   Draw up your own version of the deed. You will need to include:

● what Faustus promised to give Lucifer
● what Lucifer gave Faustus in return (in detail)
● the timescale of the bargain.

Remember that this is an important document, so it needs to be written in a formal style.

I, Doctor Faustus, agree to...

2   Why do you think Faustus has to sign the deed with his own blood? (Think about what blood represents.)
3   Faustus asks 'Does my own body shrink from making this bargain?'

● What makes him say this?
● How does it hint at what will happen later in the play?

4   At the end of the play, Faustus has to face the
     consequences of his decision. The bargain must be
     fulfilled. With a partner, discuss whether you feel any
     sympathy for Faustus. Do you feel he deserves his fate?

Morality plays

Morality plays began in the Middle Ages. They were short dramas, usually performed in the streets, and based on the Church's teachings about good and bad behaviour. By the fifteenth century, morality plays were popular all over Europe. Few people could read and write, so watching plays was a way of gaining information as well as a form of entertainment.

The play, *Doctor Faustus,* was written by Christopher Marlowe in 1588, when Queen Elizabeth I was on the throne. It contained many of the features of traditional morality plays and these are still present in Geraldine McCaughrean's retelling.

Look at the grid below. In the first column is a list of features usually found in morality plays. With a partner, decide which of these features appear in *Doctor Faustus*. Fill in the second column with examples.

Morality plays	Doctor Faustus
The main theme is about choices between good and bad behaviour.	Doctor Faustus chooses to study magic, working with forces of evil rather than forces of good.
The main character is called 'Christian' or 'Everyman'.	
We are told about his life, from birth to death.	
The main character is tempted to pursue pleasure, material wealth and power, rather than a frugal, hard-working Christian life.	
Angels and devils fight over the man's soul – angels want him to go to Heaven, with God; devils want him to go to Hell, with Lucifer.	
Other characters represent qualities (vices or virtues), e.g. Greed, Envy, Good Deeds.	
There are some comic scenes with clownish behaviour as well as more serious scenes.	
A chorus comments on events.	
The main character triumphs over temptation and his soul goes to heaven.	

A simple or complex character?

Most morality plays had simple characters – they were either good or bad. But is Doctor Faustus a simple character?

1   In a group, discuss whether Doctor Faustus is:

ambitious **humble**

greedy

humorous

intelligent *brave*

determined

curious

timid

adventurous

arrogant loyal

As a group, prepare reasons for your answers. Make sure:

- everyone has a chance to give their views
- you listen carefully to each other's opinions
- someone notes what the group decides
- someone presents the group's decisions.

2   You have probably concluded that Doctor Faustus is a complex character (unlike characters in traditional morality plays). Some people describe him as 'tragic' and the play as a 'tragedy'. Look up these words in a dictionary and decide whether you agree with these descriptions of Doctor Faustus (the man and the play).

3   The character of Doctor Faustus is based on a real German, who died about 1540. He had a bad reputation for sorcery and excessive behaviour. Find out more about this notorious character.

4   Faustus became legendary and has been the inspiration for many stories through the ages. Find out about another retelling of the Faustus story. (It could be a play or novel.)

Faustus on trial

Dramatize a trial of Doctor Faustus to decide whether he is guilty of evil deeds, and deserves punishment, or whether he is an innocent victim. Remember that different qualities and ideals are valued in different times and societies. Follow the steps below.

Step 1
First select a judge and jury. The judge should be someone who is able to listen carefully to information and then summarize it. The jury should be a group of twelve students who will decide the fate of the accused, Faustus.

Step 2
Select a volunteer to take on the role of Faustus. He or she must stay in character throughout the trial.

Step 3
Split the remaining class into two groups: one to defend Faustus, the other to prosecute him.

Step 4
The defence should consult their 'client' and plan how to justify Faustus's behaviour. They should list arguments in favour of their client, and be prepared to offer evidence to back up these arguments (e.g. witnesses, deeds).

Here are some ideas to begin with:

> ## Faustus's defence
> Ambition and thirst for knowledge should not be condemned, but praised.
> Giving in to temptation is something everyone does at some time in their lives.
> Faustus did try to repent in the end, but ...

Step 5

The prosecution should plan their arguments to persuade the court that Faustus is guilty and should be punished.

Here are some ideas to begin with:

> ### Faustus's prosecution
>
> Faustus had free choice and could have resisted temptation.
>
> Faustus was motivated by greed for wealth and power.
>
> Faustus used his power irresponsibly.

Step 6

Call Faustus to the stand. The prosecution and defence choose a 'barrister' from their group to question him, in turn. The accused must answer in character.

Step 7

Witnesses may be called to give evidence, e.g. The Old Man, Wagner, Valdes.

Step 8

The judge should sum up the situation and evidence.

Step 9

The jury discuss the case, and then decide whether Faustus is innocent or guilty.

A new comic scene

Doctor Faustus explores some very serious issues, such as right and wrong behaviour, temptation, and life after death. However, it also includes comic scenes, to give some light relief and make the audience laugh. These scenes also show how Faustus misuses his special powers, to make fools of people and play tricks on them.

Reread Act 3, Scene 2. After Bruno is 'spirited out of Rome', Faustus and Mephistopheles amuse themselves by playing tricks on the Pope and Cardinals. Afterwards, one of the chorus comments, 'His sights set upon fame and enlightenment, he steals a bite of bread, a slurp of wine ...'. With a partner, talk about what this means, i.e. the difference between what Faustus planned to do with his new powers and what he actually does.

Now look at Act 3, Scene 3. Faustus humiliates Benvolio as a punishment for mocking his magic. The Emperor feels that Faustus goes too far, and asks him to stop. Faustus says it is 'a joke, that's all', and Mephistopheles describes it as 'a moment's harmless entertainment'. But is it? Look at what Faustus and Mephistopheles say after that. Do you think:

- that Faustus feels ashamed?
- that Faustus thinks he really will do more important things with his powers?
- that Mephistopholes believes Faustus?

In small groups, invent another comic scene in which Faustus uses his powers for trivial entertainment.

1 First brainstorm ideas for a setting and outline of events. For example, the setting might be in a church, a street, a university lecture theatre, or a classroom. The events could be triggered by someone offending or challenging Faustus.

2   Choose who will play Faustus, Mephistopheles, and the other characters.

3   Decide who will play the Chorus (to comment on Faustus's actions after the event).

4   Improvise the scene, or write a script for it and then perform it in front of the class.

5   After the performance, discuss it with the audience. Talk about:

- how Faustus was portrayed
- how Mephistopheles was portrayed
- whether it was funny
- whether the Chorus made a serious point about Faustus's behaviour.

Writing a persuasive letter

Imagine you are either a good angel or a bad angel. If you are a good angel, write a letter to God to persuade Him that Faustus should be forgiven and allowed to go to Heaven. If you are a bad angel, write a letter to Lucifer to justify why Faustus should go to Hell.

Remember that when you write a persuasive text, you need to convince the reader of your viewpoint. One way of doing this is to use persuasive devices, such as:

- repetition
- rhetorical questions
- emotive language
- patterns of three
- direct address to the audience (using the second-person form of the verb, 'you')
- imperatives (commands).

You also need to argue your case clearly, linking together ideas logically, so that the audience can follow your train of thought.

Follow these steps to write your letter:

Step 1
Jot down some ideas that you want to express.

Step 2
Order your ideas into a logical sequence.

Step 3
Plan out your paragraphs. Remember to start your letter with an introduction and finish with a conclusion.

Step 4
Write the first draft of your letter. Use topic sentences at the beginning of each paragraph.

Step 5
Think carefully about how to sign off your letter. What tone and level of formality might be most effective?

Step 6
Give your draft to a partner for their comments. Ask them:

- Does this letter persuade you to share my viewpoint?
- Does it appeal to your emotions and common sense?
- Is the tone and level of formality appropriate?
- Which is the most effective part?
- Which part could be improved?

Step 7
Edit your work. This might involve:

- rephrasing text if it is not clear
- checking spellings and punctuation
- varying the length of sentences (short, memorable sentences often have the greatest impact).

Step 8
Write a final copy of your letter. If possible, write the letter on a computer. Remember:

- use the spellchecker
- use a thesaurus if you have repeated a word and want to find an alternative
- use italics or bold for emphasis.

A dramatic ending

A successful story needs to grab the audience's attention at the beginning, and then hold them in suspense until the end. In *Doctor Faustus*, the plot pivots on the choice that Faustus makes in the first scene. After that, Faustus and the audience continually question whether he has made the right choice, and whether he can change his mind. This question keeps the audience in suspense, right until the end.

The bargain sets a deadline for the resolution – twenty-four years from the day that Faustus signs it. The playwright uses this to increase tension towards the end of the play. Faustus and the audience are continually reminded of the passage of time.

1   Skim through the play to find the main references to time. They might be spoken references or props. Note down the references in a grid like the one below, where a few examples are in place.

Location in play	The time reference
Act 1, Scene 5, page 22	An hourglass is almost empty, showing that Faustus is running out of time in which he must make a decision.
Act 1, Scene 5, page 23	Faustus signs the deed giving him 24 years of service from Mephistopheles.
Act 3, Scene 2, pages 37 and 41	At the Papal Palace, Faustus says he wants 'to use every single hour and afternoon and day and week filling my head with sights and scenes!' The Chorus comment 'the years run down like sand'.

2   Draw a rough graph, showing how the references to time increase towards the end of the play. Copy the graph below, and draw in the line to show the references to time.

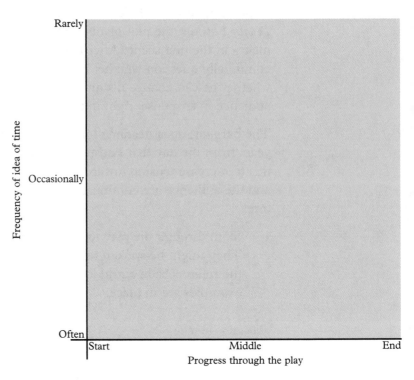

3   How does the playwright use time to increase the drama at the climax of the play?

4   In pairs or small groups, discuss other ways of conveying the passage of time in a play. Compile a list of your ideas. It might begin like this:

The use of a sun dial

Change of scenery to show passage of seasons

Change of lighting to show ...

Inventing a moral tale

Doctor Faustus is about the consequences of ambition and greed. Many stories are based on similar themes, showing how people ultimately get what they deserve.

1 In small groups, brainstorm some ideas for another moral story. You might wish to jot down your ideas in the form of a spider diagram, using the outline below.

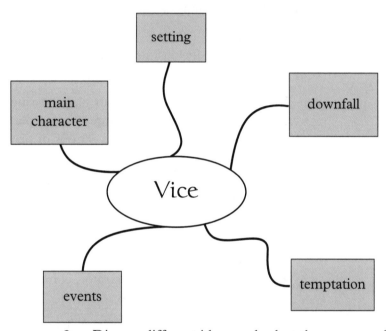

2 Discuss different ideas and select the ones you feel are the best.

3 Plot a rough outline of your story.

The beginning

This needs to grab the reader's attention, so try to think of a dramatic opening. For example, an important choice has to be made, a crisis has to be faced, two people have a serious argument, or someone is tempted to do something which they know is wrong.

The middle

The plot develops and the story unfolds, showing the main character further along their chosen route. Think about how you can indicate whether the route seems to be a good one or not.

The crisis

The main character faces danger, or a challenge, which provokes extreme emotion. Maybe he or she has to make another choice between pursuing the original goal or safeguarding something which he or she values.

The resolution

The ending should feel justified, depending on what you feel your main character deserves.

4   Write the opening scene of your play, bearing in mind the number of people in your group who can play the parts. Don't forget the following conventions of playscripts:

- stage directions convey the setting, briefly
- character names (cues) are ranged left and their words are ranged right
- stage directions indicate any props that are needed
- stage directions advise actors how to move and speak certain lines
- a chorus can act as a narrator, commenting on events.

5   Perform your scene in front of the class.

- After the performance ask your audience if they could identify the main character's weakness or vice.
- How do they predict the play will unfold? Compare it with your own version. Note that if your play is entirely predictable, you will need to add some unexpected twists to the plot!

Further activities

1 Reseach the life of Christopher Marlowe and write a short biography. Use the following headings:

- Birthday (it was shared with another famous playwright)
- Life as a spy
- Work in London
- The duel
- Arrest
- Death

2 Use a dictionary to look up the following words: 'pentacle', 'allegory', 'despair'. Write a short definition of each (in your own words) and explain how they relate to the play *Doctor Faustus*.

3 Discuss the idea of Hell. Use the playscript to find descriptions of Hell – where and what it is. Then also do this for the idea of Heaven.

- In the prologue of Marlowe's play, Faustus is compared to the Greek character, Icarus. Explore the myth of Icarus and explain how it is similar to Faustus's story.
- Some critics have described Faustus as a 'Renaissance man'. Find out what this means and write a short paragraph about whether you think it is a suitable description for Faustus.
- Consider the sub-plot in *Doctor Faustus*. How does it echo the main plot?

OXFORD Playscripts

Across the Barricades; Joan Lingard, adapted by David Ian Neville

Brother in the Land; Robert Swindells, adapted by Joe Standerline

Johnny and the Dead; Terry Pratchett, adapted by Stephen Briggs

The Amazing Maurice and his Educated Rodents; Terry Pratchett, adapted by Stephen Briggs

The Snake-stone; adapted from her own novel by Berlie Doherty

The Turbulent Term of Tyke Tiler; adapted from her own novel by Gene Kemp

The Demon Headmaster; Gillian Cross, adapted by Adrian Flynn

The Canterbury Tales; Geoffrey Chaucer, adapted by Martin Riley

Dracula; Bram Stoker, adapted by David Calcutt

Dr Faustus; Christopher Marlowe, adapted by Geraldine McCaughrean

Frankenstein; Mary Shelley, adapted by Philip Pullman

Lady Macbeth; David Calcutt

The Valley of Fear; Arthur Conan Doyle, adapted by Adrian Flynn

Troy 24; David Calcutt

The White Rose and the Swastika; Adrian Flynn

Salem; David Calcutt

For more information or to request your inspection copy of any of the Playscripts titles, please call customer services on +44 (0) 1536 741068